Meet the employees of
Deadly Force, Inc.

Luke Simpson: Founder and president. Vietnam Vet, ex-cop, former CIA, he got tired of playing by the rules. Now, this deadly soldier of fortune picks the job—and calls the shots.

Jake O'Bannion: Management and services. This hard-nosed ex-New York City cop is the caretaker of Deadly Force's HQ on Superstition Mountain. And his fighting skills are more than lethal.

Ben Sanchez: Warrior-for-hire. He fought with the Rangers in Nam. Now, this silent Apache is a part-time mercenary—and one of the deadliest on Simpson's team.

Tran Cao: Science and technology. Toughened by the war in his homeland, this sharp-witted South Vietnamese can master the world's most advanced computers—and most devastating weapons.

Calvin Steeples: Chief pilot. He was a flier in Nam. Now, he's a cropduster—when he's not helping Simpson destroy more dangerous vermin.

Deadly Force

The DEADLY FORCE Series
published by Berkley Books

DEADLY FORCE
SPECIAL DELIVERY
HEARTLANDERS

DEADLY FORCE

Heartlanders

Mark Dixon

B

BERKLEY BOOKS, NEW YORK

DEADLY FORCE: HEARTLANDERS

A Berkley Book/published by arrangement with
the author

PRINTING HISTORY
Berkley edition/March 1988

ISBN: 0-425-10691-8

A BERKLEY BOOK ® TM 757,375
Berkley Books are published by The Berkley Publishing Group,
200 Madison Avenue, New York, NY 10016.
The name "BERKLEY" and the "B" logo
are trademarks belonging to Berkley Publishing Corporation.

PRINTED IN THE UNITED STATES OF AMERICA

10   9   8   7   6   5   4   3   2   1

CHAPTER 1

Like a flash of summer lightning, the headlights speared into the dark, splashing on green leaves, then winking off. The driver grunted with satisfaction. There could be no mistaking it now; they were even closer than he had figured. The phosphorescent blue-and-white sign, OZARK ARMORY, 9, had glowed like a beacon, just long enough for him to read it. Nine miles. That wasn't bad. They had covered nearly a hundred in under three hours. On such winding roads, through an intermittent downpour, that was damn good driving. He smiled, as proud as a Little Leaguer after his first home run.

"You can put away that damn map, Randall. I told you we were heading right. You see that fucking sign?"

"I seen it. So what? We ain't there yet. You still got nine miles to get lost in."

The driver grinned. He stepped on the clutch and gunned the engine as they coasted downhill. "I'll get you lost, all right. Get your ass so damn lost, even your mama won't find you."

Randall punched the driver on the arm. It wasn't a playful gesture.

" 'Less you can drive a rig like this, Randall, you better quit it."

1

"Shit, ain't nothing to it, Jimbo. Truck like this? Damn near drives its own self."

"You think so? Here . . ."

Jimbo opened the driver's door and stepped out onto the running board. He let go of the wheel, and Randall grabbed it frantically, sliding over to sit behind it. He spat out the open door and cursed at the grinning driver. The truck lurched over the narrow road, the trees at either side a mass of dull shadow soaking up the dim orange glow of the parking lights.

"What the hell are you doin', Jimbo? You crazy? Get in here and take this damn wheel."

Jimbo swung back into the truck as Randall slid over to the passenger side to make room for him. Before he could answer, the canvas flap behind their seat slapped open. An angry face appeared in the opening.

"You assholes better quit clowning around. This ain't no hayride. I tell Akins about this, he'll hand you both your asses. And it won't be on no platter, neither."

"Just having a little fun, Marcelli. Why don't you loosen up?" Jimbo sounded more angry than contrite. It wasn't lost on Marcelli.

"I told Akins you were a worthless son of a bitch. I told you that, too, didn't I?"

"Ever' chance you got, Marcelli."

"Yeah, well . . ." The flap rippled, and the face disappeared.

Jimbo reopened his door to pull it shut with a loud bang.

"I hope the dumb shit fell out," somebody yelled from the back of the truck.

Jimbo didn't dignify the remark with an answer. The truck picked up speed, its big diesel whining. The twin stacks belched smoke and noise up and over the canvas cover, drowning out any further remarks from the truck bed.

Randall watched the driver curiously. He wanted to ask Jimbo a question, but it was the first time in the whole trip the driver had been quiet. Randall decided to relax and enjoy it.

Five minutes later the forest to their right thinned out a little. Randall could see the patterned shadow of a chain-link fence five yards off the road, threading its way through the rippling vegetation.

Jimbo leaned forward to peer at the dim lights on the dash. The odometer rolled slowly ahead. He watched the numbers for a minute, then disengaged the gears, coasting to a stop in a small clearing just off the shoulder.

He turned to the canvas flap, pulled it to one side, and leaned into the back. "We're here."

Leaving the engine running, he opened the door and jumped down, his feet squishing in the damp grass. He bent over and swiped at some mud on the toe of one combat boot, gleaming in the orange light. Straightening, he walked to the rear of the truck, his starched, neatly pressed fatigues whispering stiffly.

Four men were already on the ground, three of them busily smearing black cream on their faces, hands, and necks. A moment later Randall joined them.

Marcelli watched them quietly. They had practiced this a hundred times, but he still wasn't convinced they knew what they were doing. They were a bunch of rawboned fuck-ups, as far as he was concerned, better suited to a barroom brawl on a Saturday night than anything remotely military. Their sun-darkened faces and red necks disappeared under the night cream, but they were still undisciplined crackers.

Marcelli stepped into the thin stand of trees back away from the road and leaned against the wire fence. He had a bad feeling about the night's operation. Practice was one thing; disciplined execution of a calculated, precisely timed maneuver was something else again. He didn't doubt their intentions, just their skills. He had argued with Akins about it, but once the chief made up his mind, there was no changing it. Priding himself on his flexibility and his willingness to accept the command structure, like any good soldier was supposed to, Marcelli had acquiesced. But the capitulation had done nothing to quiet his misgivings.

When the men had finished daubing themselves, he bounced away from the fence without using his hands and stepped back to the truck.

"You all know what you're supposed to do, right?"

The chorus of acknowledgment sounded halfhearted and less than certain.

"You want me to run through it one more time?"

"Marcelli, give it a rest, would you? You ain't a sergeant anymore, and this ain't no army," Jimbo snapped.

The fist flashed out without warning, catching the driver on the left cheek, just under the eye. He went down in a heap. "Anybody else got anything to say?" When no one did, Marcelli turned away from them abruptly. "Get your asses in the truck. Randall, you get in the back. I think I'm going to have to keep an eye on our resident smartass, here."

Marcelli waited until he heard the canvas yanked shut, then walked to the front of the truck. He was sitting quietly when Jimbo climbed in behind the wheel. The driver was a dozen years younger and outweighed him by thirty pounds. He watched Jimbo's thick wrists as the driver adjusted his seat and reached for the gearshift. He said nothing. He knew he didn't have to.

The truck lurched back onto the macadam, its big tires hissing on the slick pavement.

"All right, Jimbo, put on your headlights."

The driver clicked them on without speaking.

"And let me do the talking. You just drive, okay?"

Jimbo nodded. Even in the dim light of the cab Marcelli could see the angry red of his neck and cheeks. Popping him one had been a calculated risk. Whether it would do Jimbo any good was debatable, he knew, but at least it would keep the others in line. Until the first beer, anyway.

A pair of stone pillars materialized out of the darkness, the heavy iron gates between them closed and, as expected, chained shut. A sentry box stood to the left. Marcelli could see two men inside. They ignored the truck for a minute, and Marcelli leaned over to tap the horn button.

One of the sentries looked annoyed, shaking his head as he got to his feet. The other said something, and they both laughed soundlessly. The first man stepped out, looking up at the sky for a few seconds before crossing to the driver's door.

"You fellows lost?" he asked.

Marcelli leaned toward him. "No, got a pickup to make."

"Wait a minute." The guard stepped back to the sentry box and returned with a clipboard in his hand. "Nothing here about a pickup. Everything's accounted for."

"Here's the order," Marcelli said. He handed the thick sheaf of multicolored NCR paper through the window.

The guard skimmed it quickly, then handed it back. "Looks okay to me. Wait a second while I get the keys." He stepped to the box and yanked a sliding window open. The other sentry handed him a heavy key ring, and he walked over to the thick chain securing the gates.

When the lock was free, he shoved one rollered gate aside and walked the other back away from the truck. He stepped back to the driver's side. "Hope you know where the stuff is. Nobody's likely to be around to help you find it. Most everybody's in town tonight. Warehouse you want is the last one on the right. You have any trouble, Lieutenant Mason's the OD. He'll be in the main office, at the other end." He gestured toward a long, narrow, one-story building, its white clapboard starkly etched by several overhead lamps.

"That's all right, we'll manage. Sorry we're so late. We broke down on the way out."

"You want to use the phone to call in?"

"No thanks. Already took care of it."

The sentry stepped aside. Jimbo popped the clutch, the gears protesting as the engine rumbled. He glanced at the side-view mirror and grunted. "Asshole is leaving the gate open, just like we figured."

The truck lumbered down the broad asphalt strip, broken by speed bumps every fifteen yards or so. "Coming out, I think we better drive on the grass," Jimbo said.

"No way. We do this by the book, Jimbo."

"Book? What book? What the fuck is this book you're always talking about? Shit!"

"I'd show it to you," Marcelli said, "but you're an illiterate country boy, can't read nohow." He mimicked Jimbo's drawl, much to the driver's annoyance.

"You know, Marcelli, one day you and me are really going to have it out."

"Anytime, Jimbo, anytime."

"The sooner the better, you ask me."

"Shut up and drive."

Jimbo lapsed into silence. The warehouse loomed ahead, its main door lit by a single bulb on a fixture mounted over its center. The truck bounced into a tight circle, then backed toward the corrugated door. Marcelli jumped out and punched a code into the electronic lock. When it clicked open, he pressed the rectangular red button with his thumb, watching the door roll heavily up and away from the opening. He stepped in and felt for the light switch. Finding it, he clicked it on, and the interior of the cavernous building was flooded with harsh white light.

He walked backward into the warehouse, waving his arms like a traffic cop. The truck followed, like a puppet on invisible wires. At the far end of the building he stopped. Ripping aside the canvas flap, he called into the truck. "Let's go, let's go. We don't have all night."

The four men, three in blackface, jumped down and waited for further instructions.

Marcelli pulled a sheet of folded paper from his shirt pocket and glanced at it. "Okay, here's what we need. Now let's get it in gear and load up. You two, start right here. I want eight cases of M16s. Then get as much ammo as you can. And make sure it's M16 ammo! You two, come with me."

He stepped down a narrow aisle, mountains of crated weapons towering above him on either side. He pointed out items from his inventory list, and two men scurried back and forth, lugging the heavy crates. In thirty minutes, they were finished. The truck rode low on its springs down a narrow aisle. Marcelli ran to the cab and jumped in.

"Let's go, Jimbo. Stop just outside the door."

"Piece of cake, wasn't it?"

"So far."

The truck lurched down the aisle, its laboring engine reverberating among the steel girders fifty feet above. At the door, Marcelli jumped out and switched off the lights. He punched the button to close the door, and hopped back into the cab before it touched down.

"Remember, nothing fancy, now. Just take it easy until we get through the gate and out of sight."

"Shit, nothing to worry about. Them clowns don't suspect a thing."

He started rolling forward, the truck's groaning as he cleared each speed bump. As they neared the gate Marcelli noticed one of the sentries on the phone.

"Uh-oh!"

"Forget it, he's talking to some broad, prob'ly."

Before Marcelli could answer, the other sentry sprinted out and began to haul the gate shut. Through the window he saw the first guard slam down the phone. A moment later he appeared in the gateway, his rifle held loosely in one hand. The guard raised the rifle, signaling them to stop.

"Be cool, Jimbo."

The driver ignored the warning, gunning the engine and shifting down. The guard reacted immediately, dropping to one knee. He sighted rapidly, letting go with a quick burst that showered sparks from the asphalt in front of the truck. Jimbo slammed on the brakes.

The guard remained on one knee while his companion warily approached the truck, his own rifle aimed, almost casually, toward the cab.

"What the hell are you guys doing?"

"Stay right there, mister. Don't fucking move or you're history."

The windshield shattered with a roar, and the advancing guard fell to the asphalt, blood turning the water, lit by the truck's headlights, bright pink, then darker and darker red. The other sentry dived for cover, but a second burst of fire from the rear of the truck slammed into his thigh, and he fell heavily, his fatigue pants already stained with a bright, sticky red.

Marcelli jumped down from the running board and approached the fallen man. A hand took him by the shoulder and tossed him roughly aside. Marcelli fell, landing on his right shoulder and smacking his head into the pavement, momentarily stunned. He shook his head to clear it. Three rapid shots from a handgun echoed off into the night as he was getting to his feet.

Jimbo holstered his .45 automatic. "Son of a bitch could have identified us. Let's roll."

CHAPTER 2

The thermometer read 120 degrees. Luke Simpson stared at the red column in disbelief. He knew all the clichés about Arizona heat being easier to take, but dry heat was still heat, and 120 degrees was hot by any standard.

It was too hot to bother with paperwork. He propped his feet up on the patio railing and looked out over the desert. The bands of color shimmered in the convection currents, and high overhead a hawk rode the rising air, beating its wings every so often to stabilize its flight. As the chief executive officer of Deadly Force, Inc., it was his prerogative to take it easy. Despite his natural inclination to work longer hours and get more done than any two ordinary men, today was his exception. Today he was going to exercise his executive privilege.

He stared vacantly at the pool, fifty yards below on the slope beneath the house. An extensive collection of native cacti nearly screened it from view, but glints of blue flashed here and there among gaps in the spiny wall. He knew the water would be warm, more like a bath than a swimming pool, but anything was preferable to baking in the sun or, worse yet, huddling in the dark, artificial coolness of the air-conditioned interior of the compound.

Luke walked indoors and slipped on a pair of bathing trunks. At a tad over 6', 190 pounds, he was in great shape. His twenties were more than a little behind him, but he'd never been in better shape. Taking care of himself came naturally. You don't spend time on a SWAT team, let alone in the jungles of Southeast Asia—both of which had taught Luke a few hard lessons—if you didn't watch your ass. And watching your ass, for a man approaching middle age, meant watching your calories, your cholesterol, and your EKG. Luke wasn't a health nut, but he wouldn't mind living his full three score and ten, so he did what the doctor told everyone to do.

Grabbing a robe of elaborately embroidered Japanese silk and slipping it on over his trunks, Luke walked to the elevator, which took him down through three floors of the Deadly Force complex, and stepped out into a private corridor leading to the pool area. Moving out into the heat again, he began to have second thoughts when a tremendous splash seized his attention.

Luke broke into the open, past the wall of cactus; just as the source of the commotion broke the surface, spluttering and swinging great arcs of water from its longish black hair. The last surviving master of the cannonball, Jake O'Bannion, had just tossed forty gallons of water onto the terra-cotta tiles at poolside with what could only have been a 9.9. The Greg Louganis of the downscale dives, Jake loved to flounder around and took every opportunity to avail himself of the pool.

Luke watched silently as Jake fell backward in the water, his slight paunch breaking the surface as he floated with closed eyes and launched a spout of chlorinated water high into the air.

Luke slipped off his robe and took a running leap, landing five feet to Jake's left and sending a tidal wave in the direction of his unsuspecting second-in-command. Still under water, Luke could hear Jake cursing him and three generations of his forebears. He surfaced laughing, and O'Bannion renewed his invective with considerable splashing of his own.

"You son of a bitch, Simpson. You scared the living bejesus out of me."

"I meant to, Jake. You were too tempting a target."

"You'll regret it—and the day you were born, as well. What are you doing down here, anyway? I thought you had all that paperwork to do."

"I do, but it's been quiet for a couple of days, and the paperwork isn't going anyplace. Besides, I figured if the help can frolic in the pool, I have the same privileges."

"But you have responsibilities. You should set a good example for the rest of us."

"Later. Right now I'm going to relax a little. Hell, I might even knock back a beer or two and cook some burgers on the patio."

"Now you're talking. What time do we eat?"

"Around three or—" The poolside phone interrupted him. He looked at Jake and shook his head.

"Don't answer it, lad," Jake said. "We've got enough to do as it is."

Luke ignored the older man's advice and did a quick crawl to the edge of the pool. Hauling himself up onto the terracotta border, he reached for the phone as it rang a fifth time.

"Hello?"

Jake rolled over and watched, drifting slowly away from the talking man as he floated across the pool.

"Yeah. All right, I'll be right up."

Luke listened for a moment, and then Jake heard what he had hoped not to hear. "Yeah, he's down here. Okay. Right. Ten minutes."

Luke replaced the receiver. As he turned to fill Jake in, the latter, with whalelike grace, rolled over and dug in, heading straight for the bottom of the pool, flipping his impossibly pale Gaelic feet like diminutive flukes. When he surfaced, spluttering, Luke was leaning over the edge of the pool.

"Sorry, Jake. We've got company."

"I'm afraid to ask."

"Somebody from Army intelligence."

"Isn't that a contradiction in terms?"

"That's amusing, but it won't get you off the hook. Come on, old sport, let's go."

Luke tilted back in the well-worn leather chair behind his desk. He reached for the intercom, and a moment later the office door opened. Jake sat in one corner, trying his best to be invisible. Janice, the new assistant, ushered in the visitor.

"Colonel David Milford, this is Luke Simpson." She withdrew with a flutter of upturned hands, as if to say she hadn't a clue what the colonel wanted.

Luke stood and grasped the colonel's outstretched hand. "The man sulking in the corner is Jake O'Bannion, my EO. Colonel, what can we do for you?"

"I'm not sure. Let me tell you what has prompted my visit, and you tell me whether you think you can be of service."

"Fair enough. Can I offer you something to drink before we begin?"

"Thank you, no. I don't have very much time. I'm due in Dallas this evening."

"All right, I'll stop interrupting you, then."

"Three days ago there was an unauthorized removal of weapons and ammunition from the Ozark Armory. I won't waste time with the inventory. It's all here," Milford said, patting a large manila envelope he removed from his briefcase. "If we go any further with this, I'll leave the papers for you to examine."

"When you say 'unauthorized removal,' what you mean is that they were stolen, am I right?"

"Perhaps. We're not certain. The men who participated in the . . . removal were carrying appropriate papers. Everything was in order, the proper authorization numbers, the date-coding, everything. The only thing out of the ordinary is that the officer who signed the papers doesn't exist. That is, he couldn't have signed the papers, because he's been dead for more than a year."

"You're joking." Luke sat forward in his chair. "That's not possible."

"I am well aware of that, Mr. Simpson. But nevertheless

it's true. Unfortunately two young men were killed by the thieves, if that is what they were."

"Why should there be any doubt about that?"

"Because, as you are well aware, there are many hands in Washington. None knows everything the others may be up to."

"Can't you double-check? There can't be too many agencies that might be involved in something like this."

"Under ordinary circumstances, yes. But since the young men, two sentries, were killed, it is doubtful that the agency responsible, if indeed there is one, will now admit it. For obvious reasons."

"Forgive me if I am not exactly sympathetic with that reasoning, Colonel."

"I understand. Off the record, I don't believe this was authorized by any branch of the intelligence services of this country. My own particular belief is that some sort of renegade cabal of officers might be involved. Somebody in a position to forge those papers successfully, and the dead officer's signature, had to be plugged into a fairly high echelon of the military."

"And does your theory go so far as to include possible suspects?"

"Not by name, only by profile."

Luke was getting very interested. "Go on, please." He lit a cigarette and offered the pack to the colonel, who declined with a shake of his head. "I can establish a limited range of possibility, perhaps even a probability array. Unfortunately the number of candidates is still several hundred, and they're scattered over half the globe."

"And what exactly would you like us to do?" Luke asked.

"Recover the weapons."

"That's all?"

"It is not an easy assignment, I know," Milford said, ignoring Luke's sarcasm. "But we have reason to believe those weapons were taken for some specific purpose. It was not just a random theft."

"Are you speaking for yourself now or for your agency?"

"Both. I have succeeded in persuading General Wilson of my position."

"Am I to understand that General Wilson agrees with you, or merely that he does not have sufficient evidence to rule out the possibility you suggest?"

"There is no practical difference between the two."

"On the contrary, Colonel, on the contrary. I am not unacquainted with the bureaucratic foibles of intelligence agencies."

"I'm afraid I don't know what you're driving at."

"It's simple, really. If General Wilson, whom I happen to know and for whom I have little regard, cannot rule out your suspicion, he has to let you follow your inclination to cover his own ass. But he doesn't have to help you in your investigation, or me in mine, should I decide to accept the assignment you are proposing. I will bat one-handed, Colonel, but I'll be damned if I'll also wear a blindfold."

"I appreciate your candor, Mr. Simpson. And you are quite right. General Wilson is extremely reluctant to permit me to mount this investigation. And it is unlikely that he will cooperate in any substantive way. He'll observe the barest formal obligations, and little more."

"And what about you, Colonel? What sort of assistance can you render?"

"Little enough, I'm afraid. On the other hand, I'm not without certain bureaucratic resources of my own. They are no match for the general's superior clout, obviously. But there are a number of other officers in Army intelligence who are concerned enough about this situation that we can, as a group, get you considerably more assistance than I first believed."

"Why me, Colonel? Why Deadly Force, Inc.?"

"I know your reputation. I also know you are not one to accept a simple no from those in authority when you suspect the truth is otherwise."

"Are you suggesting I'm a pain in the ass?"

"I'm suggesting you have the ability to be, when it suits your purpose. And I think that may very well be necessary if this situation is to be expeditiously resolved."

"You'll accept my conclusions, if I can substantiate them?"

"Yes."

"And I have your assurance that the evidence will not be deep-sixed if it is unpleasant for persons of influence?"

"To the best of my ability, yes."

"All right, let me think about it."

"There's very little time, I'm afraid. I have to have an answer before I leave."

"And so you shall. Why don't you tell me everything you have learned so far?"

"May I take it you are seriously considering accepting the assignment?"

"You may do more than that, Colonel. You may take it that I have already accepted it. All I want to do now is convince myself I haven't made a bad decision."

Jake sighed. Getting up from his chair, he said, "Here, give us a gander at those papers, Colonel." He did not look happy.

CHAPTER 3

The sun seemed low enough to touch. The temperature was nearly 100 degrees, and it was still only eleven o'clock. Thick dust, kicked up by hundreds of restless feet, hung in the air like a dry fog, collecting on faded coveralls and turning to fine mud on sweating arms and necks.

The roar of conversation grew louder with every diesel arriving. For miles around, pickups and vans clogged the highways, adding their exhaust to the already oppressive air. Jason Macalester counted plates from eleven states, including two from Texas and one from Mississippi. Most of the crowd couldn't have cared less what states, or how many, were represented. But then, most of the crowd wasn't Jason Macalester, or, like Jason, sheriff of Downing County.

Macalester moved casually through the throng, nodding occasionally, shaking a hand here and there, even smiling once or twice at a familiar face. There were far too few of the latter to his way of thinking, and he was conscious of the angry undertone running through the crowd like a high-voltage current looking for someplace to go.

Macalester pushed his stained Stetson back on his head and hauled a thick blue-and-white-checkered handkerchief from his black pocket. He swiped at his brow, feeling the sticky grit against his skin like a jeweler's paste or rubbing compound. He shook the cloth and wiped a second time.

The ominous buzz grew louder as a small convoy of pickups turned off the shimmering asphalt of County Road 391 and rocked across the sunbaked furrows of an open field at the far edge of the crowd. Macalester stood on tiptoe, craning his neck for a glimpse of Wiley Johnson or Andy Travis. The deputies, like their boss, were working the crowd. It made Macalester uneasy to have so little help, but he only had four deputies, and somebody would have to take the night shift, so he'd have to make do with two. They were both good men, but an angry crowd was only an inch or two short of a mob. The ugly mood was only going to worsen as the sun, and the temperature, rose higher.

When the rally started, it wouldn't take much of a spark to blow the whole powder keg sky high. Macalester had read about similar rallies in other states. What he knew about them didn't do much to inspire confidence. Farmers in general were in a tough spot. Those in hock up to their necks were mad as hell. Everybody else was frightened they were next. That morning's rally, ostensibly to protest the foreclosure auction of Matt Winslow's farm, heavy equipment, house, and everything in it, was more likely a futile exercise in intimidation.

Grasping at straws, those on the verge of following Winslow under the surging flood of debt were flexing their flaccid economic muscles in the naïve hope that the bank could be persuaded to cut Winslow a little slack. Any banker you talked to said the same thing; the slack was long since paid out, the rope stretched to the breaking point. When it came down to it, as Macalester well knew, a lifeline was as good as a noose for a hanging. All it needed was somebody to kick the chair out from under you. And that, as Macalester also knew, was what most farmers thought the banks were doing.

Marshall Akins was the unknown in the heady brew simmering under the sweltering sun. His reputation, mysteriously incomplete and comprised as much of rumor as of fact, was formidable. And it had preceded him to Downing County. As word spread that he was going to lead the protest, excitement started to run through any small gathering in town. Macalester noticed how small knots of men whispered together, peeking over their shoulders like schoolboys hatching a plot. When he got close, they leaned back, raising their voices in greetings more effusive than sincere. When he passed on by, he glanced back and they'd all be leaning in again, whispering.

Some of the talk, he knew, was hot air. But Marshall Akins was the kind of man who seemed to extract more than just hot air from heads full of little else.

Jason had wanted to bar the rally altogether. Stanley Jefferson, the president of Downing Savings and Loan, had also wanted it cancelled. And since Jefferson also happened to be chairman of the Board of County Supervisors, and therefore the man who signed his paychecks, Macalester had felt considerable pressure. But a check with the state attorney general had confirmed the worst: There were no legal grounds for canceling the rally. All he could do was keep an eye on Akins and, if he stepped over the line, wherever the hell that was, toss him in the can overnight.

Macalester felt a tug on the back of his shirt. He turned slowly, tilting his hat forward. Matt Winslow teetered unsteadily, his coveralls caked with dust. His blue work shirt was damp under the arms. He was hatless, and his forehead seemed to glow a dark pink under the harsh sun.

"Came for a tractor, Sheriff?" Winslow's words were slurred. He obviously had been hitting the juice.

Macalester smiled sadly. "Matt, how you holding up?"

"Ain't me holding up, Sheriff. I'm the one's bein' held up. There a reward for Stanley Jefferson? I'll bring him in myself. which fender you drape a dead banker over?"

"Matt, you don't want to be talking like that, not even in fun."

"You think this is fun, Sheriff? You ever stood around and watched everything you ever worked for wrapped up and hauled away, like you was already dead and buried?"

"I know how you feel, Matt, I truly do. But—"

"No buts, Sheriff. No damn buts about it. I'm finished. Weren't for Louise and the kids, I'd get my shotgun and—"

"No, you wouldn't. You wouldn't do that, Matt. You have too much sense."

"Sense? No damn use having sense if you don't have dollars. Ain't that right, Stanley? Dollars and sense. Stanley?" Winslow turned precariously, raising his voice and shouting into the crowd. The noise attracted a few of the nearby farmers, mostly strangers. Winslow's neighbors were embarrassed for him, tried to ignore the man, and started edging away. Pain like Winslow's just might be contagious.

The angry farmer turned back to the lawman. "Sheriff, if Stanley Jefferson don't show up, I'll keep all this, what's mine, right? I keep it."

"I'm afraid not, Matt."

" 'Course I do. Man supposed to keep his word. He says he's going to auction your family off and he don't, then he's had his chance."

"That's not how it works, Matt. You know that."

"Jason," Winslow said with a sigh, "I don't know *what* I know anymore. All I know is I broke my ass on this farm for twenty years. Seems like I ought to have something to show for it. All that time. All that work. Hell, what good's a farmer without a farm? You tell me, Jason. You got to, because I don't know anymore." Winslow turned away.

Macalester reached out to pat him on the shoulder. "It'll work out, Matt. Everything'll be all right. You'll see."

Winslow turned back, his face twisted. He squinted in the bright sunlight flooding his features. "Jason, what am I gonna do? What the hell am I gonna do now?"

"Why don't you leave him be, Sheriff? This ain't no concern of yours."

Macalester turned. He didn't recognize the voice. A big man, his face the color of old leather, stepped forward. His clothes were too neat to be those of a working farmer. Macalester thought the man might have been dressed up for a costume party. He didn't get it quite right.

"Mind your own business, Mr. . . . ?"

"Don't matter what my name is, Sheriff. Man here is suffering. You don't have to rub his damn nose in it."

"Friend, if that's what you think I'm doing, then you got a lot to learn about me, and about the people around here."

"I doubt it. Fucking bankers are all alike. Sheriffs, too, come to that. A man ought not be ripped off his land like this. You should be ashamed of yourself. If this man is your friend, you ought to be on his side. Instead you're here to make sure the bank don't miss nothing. You going to help 'em load up the furniture too?"

A few of the others mumbled encouragement. Macalester felt uneasy. The weight of his side arm kept tugging at his hip, like a restless child trying to get his attention. He didn't like the feeling.

He started to walk away, but the big man grabbed his shoulder. Macalester turned slowly. At 6'1" and 210, Macalester wasn't a small man. But the stranger had a good three inches and twenty pounds on him. Macalester reached up and grabbed the hand on his shoulder. Under the man's leathery skin, the muscle was rock-hard. The stranger leaned forward, almost as if he were nearsighted. He, too, had been drinking.

"You know, Sheriff, we ain't going to let this happen." He turned to the others crowding in around him. "Ain't that right, fellas?"

The ugly mood was starting to crystallize. It was the last thing Macalester needed. Before he could answer, a distant siren stabbed through the brittle, dust-filled air. Macalester spotted the familiar red strobe flash of the State Police. Three cars, each carrying four troopers, nosed through the crowd, heading toward the auctioneer's podium.

"I'll see you gentlemen later," Macalester said, pushing through the tight circle toward the trooper contingent. The slam of their car doors was the only sound other than the dying moan of their sirens.

"This isn't over, Sheriff," the big man shouted.

Macalester ignored him. He spotted Royce Jones, a captain in the State Police, and made a beeline for the pudgy trooper.

"Got a real ruckus in the making, eh, Jason?" Jones smiled, but it went no deeper than his thin lips.

"The local boys are all right—a little feisty, is all. I'm not sure about the rest of them, though."

"Akins has a passel of his own groupies, seems like. They travel around with him, stir things up a little. Makes sure he gets noticed that way."

"They try anything here, they'll get more notice than they bargained for, I'll promise you that."

Jones surveyed the crowd before answering. "Looks like almost a thousand, don't it? Like to have a lemonade stand for these boys. Make a bundle."

"These fellows aren't interested in lemonade, Royce."

"Well, Akins is on his way. I passed him on the way here. Big old Lincoln, bright blue. You can't miss it. Got Texas plates, custom jobs. HARTLAND, they say. What time's the auction supposed to start?"

Macalester checked his watch. " 'Bout a half hour, give or take."

"I guess we can keep these boys under control for that long. Once the auction starts, they'll be too busy trying to get a deal on a combine to give a shit about Akins or anybody else."

"I'm not so sure, Royce."

The crowd buzzed, and Macalester craned his neck to look over the sea of John Deere caps and straw ten-gallons. "Looks like the man of the hour has arrived, Jason. Let me get my boys in place." Jones walked back to the clump of troopers standing silently together, off to one side. Macalester watched the little captain issue orders with vigorous gesticulation, and the troopers fanned out, their Smokey hats noticeable as much for their lack of dust as for their distinctive design.

A boatlike baby-blue Lincoln convertible nosed through the crowd, parking beside the police cars. A raillike man in crisply starched Army fatigues and a cowboy hat slid out of the passenger side and walked around to open the rear door on the driver's side.

The passenger stepped out of the car, his checked flannel shirt new enough to have the pinholes still in it. His jeans were tailored and discreetly faded. Behind mirrored sunglasses, the face was impassive. A tan that spoke more of a salon than sunshine gave him the look of a Hollywood celebrity.

"So. The famous Marshall Akins," Macalester whispered. "Let's just see what we have here."

CHAPTER 4

Marshall Akins stepped back from the podium to watch the portable public-address system being set up. Two speaker banks, raised above the crowd level on collapsible metal columns, were aimed at the expectant throng. A brief burst of feedback caused him to scowl at the two men assembling the system.

A voice from the back of the crowd yelled, "Give 'em hell, Marshall." A slight smile flickered across his smooth features, then he raised a hand to shield his eyes while he surveyed the assembly.

Finally one of the sound crew nodded, and Akins stepped forward. He rapped the microphone sharply, sending a dull thud off into the dusty air. He leaned in, placed a hand on either side of the podium; and scanned the crowd from left to right. He nodded occasionally as someone waved. The farmers shuffled forward, as if uncertain that the sound system would do the trick.

"I guess you all think you know why you're here. Is that right?"

"Sure do."

"Damn straight, Marshall!"

"You bet."

Macalester listened to the random responses from anonymous farmers and wondered how many of them were engineered, preplanned. He didn't recognize any of the voices. He stepped closer to the rear of the podium, keeping one eye on the crowd and watching Akins with the other.

When the noise died down, Akins leaned into the mike and whispered, "Well, you're wrong. You don't have a clue."

Angry muttering rippled through the crowd. This wasn't what they had come to hear. If they wanted to be told how dumb they were, they could talk to Stanley Jefferson, or watch the network news. Some of those in front even backed up a little, as if they had been physically assaulted. The crowd compressed, and some of those in the middle ranks had to maneuver for room.

Akins smiled. "Now hold on, I'm not saying you're stupid. I'm saying you've been lied to. Lied to by people you trust, people you think are supposed to look out for your interests. Hell, you been lied to by people you vote for, and people you've known all your lives. Believing those people doesn't make you dumb, it just makes you good Americans."

The crowd pressed forward a bit, reassured.

"Used to be," Akins continued, raising his voice like a fundamentalist preacher hitting his stride, "being a good American was enough. It was for me. It was for you."

Akins stopped again, eyeballing a few in the front row. Lowering his voice again, he resumed. "Nowadays, though, it's only good enough for the bloodsuckers and the other leeches, getting fat off you, then kicking you in the butt when you can't give any more. No, sir—nowadays, being a good American just means you're fair game. I'm here to tell you how to be better Americans, Americans like the men who make this country great in the first place. Think about it for a second . . . would George Washington sit back and let some pin-striped smoothie take Mount Vernon away from him? Would Jefferson let some New York banker foreclose on Monticello? I don't think so."

Akins stepped back from the podium. He bent out of sight for a second, took a quick pull on a glass of ice water, then straightened up again.

"And some of you out there are no damn better than those leeches I'm talkin' about. Some of you come here today to buy a man's sofa right out from under his butt. You want a good deal on the refrigerator he keeps his food in. I bet one of you would even buy his kids' toys. What are you going to pay, a penny on the dollar? That sound like a good deal to you?"

Macalester wormed his way across the back of the podium to stand beside Captain Royce Jones.

"He's a piece of work, ain't he, Jason? Makes a lot of sense, that boy does."

Macalester shook his head. "I've seen better acting on cable TV, Royce."

"That ain't no act. You watch. He knows what he's doin', and he believes in it too."

"That don't make it right. It's not hard to get people on your side if you tell them what they want to hear."

"Hell, Jason, I thought Matt Winslow was a friend of yours."

"He is."

"Don't sound like you're too worried about him."

"Matt's a good man, but he's a lousy farmer. And he drinks too damn much. If he paid as much attention to his farm as he did his liquor, none of us would be here today."

Akins cleared his throat, sending a rumble out over the rolling fields surrounding them on all sides. "You know, you ought to take a good, long look at yourselves. Then take a look at the men standing next to you. Ask yourselves if friends would do what you came here to do. Make up your minds. Would a man buy your property at bargain-basement prices if he was your friend?"

Macalester was growing uneasy. Akins was clearly leading up to something, but so far he hadn't tipped his hand as to what it might be. Members of the crowd looked at one another, then quickly looked away, most staring at the dusty ground at their feet, a few looking skyward, as if charting the progress of the sun.

"And ask yourselves another question. Stanley Jefferson is

a man you've all known for as long as you've been wearing long pants. He wouldn't screw you, would he?''

"Damn right, he would. He's a banker, ain't he?"

Macalester spotted the man who had yelled. It was the big stranger who had given him grief earlier in the morning.

"I hear you, friend," Akins said, drawing a cheer from the crowd. "But you got to look at the big picture. Stanley Jefferson wouldn't screw you, not if it was left up to him. Trouble is, it *ain't* up to him. He takes orders. You don't think for one minute Downing Savings and Loan belongs to him, do you? And it sure as hell don't belong to you, I don't give a damn how much money you got on deposit. You want to know who owns Downing Savings and Loan, you got to look somewhere else, off that way." Akins gestured in the general direction of the northeast.

"Chances are, the man lives in New York. And he probably ain't even a Christian. Which is why Christian charity is in short supply here this morning. You know, you don't have to look too far to find the truth, friends. It's right there in this book. You all should know it, but I brought it along, in case you don't." Akins thumped a well-worn book, its leather binding frayed at the edges, on the microphone.

"You hear that, friends? You want to know what that noise is, that rumble? It ain't thunder, friends. It's the voice of God, the Christian God. This is the Bible, and you all know it's the revealed word of God . . . even if Stanley Jefferson, and the men who tell him what to do, don't know it."

Akins paused again for a sip of water.

"You all remember the story of Jesus and the moneylenders. You remember what Jesus did and what he said. But in case any of you don't, I'll remind you. He drove them out of the temple and said they had made the holy place a den of thieves. Now that's just about right, isn't it? Where's Matt Winslow? Get him up here."

Atkins stepped back from the podium and looked around. One of the fatigue-clad bodyguards leaned down and grabbed an extended hand, hauling Winslow bodily up the short flight of steps.

Winslow looked bewildered. Macalester knew it was not

just alcohol that had befuddled the man. He wasn't used to so much attention, and the celebrity had him off-balance. He teetered noticeably.

Akins shook Winslow's hand, draped an arm over his shoulder, and pulled him toward the microphone. "I know Matt isn't one for public speaking. But I know what's on his mind. You all know it too. And I'll tell you what we're going to do about it. In a few minutes your Mr. Jefferson is going to come up here with a gavel in his hand. He's going to make a lot of noise hammering on this little block of wood here, and he's going to ask you to pay cash money for a piece of Matt Winslow's soul."

An angry undercurrent rippled through the crowd, now pressing closer to the podium. "But I'll tell you what we're going to do, friends. Nothing! Not a goddamn thing! Jefferson can pound this damn block to splinters, and we aren't going to say a word. When he asks how much we bid on that John Deere tractor over there, we don't say anything. When he asks how much he can get for that Dodge pickup, sitting there next to the tractor, we bite our tongues, even if we could use a good truck. And when he tells us how good this land is, we're all going to nod, maybe even agree with him out loud. But when he opens the bidding, we don't say a blessed word. And when the bidding closes, you can hear a pin drop, because nobody has offered a dime. Not one thin dime. And, friends, your silence will speak volumes. It will tell those bankers in New York, and the men in that hip pocket we call Washington, D.C., 'No thank you. We aren't interested. You can't buy and sell a man like he wasn't nothing but a cow.' And when we're done saying nothing, I guarantee you, they'll hear us. Loud and clear."

Akins stood back. The applause, sporadic at first, grew in intensity until the farmers were chanting and waving their hats in the air. When the noise died down, Akins stepped back to the microphone.

"All right, now. They wanted an auction. They wanted to sell Matt Winslow's soul to the highest bidder. I'm going to step down now and let Stanley Jefferson have a go at it. Let him try. I dare him!"

Akins left the podium, and Macalester watched him walk to the front of the crowd, taking a place right below the podium. Three guards surrounded him, facing outward, toward the crowd behind him.

Stanley Jefferson climbed up to the platform. As he took a last look at the papers on his clipboard, Macalester couldn't help but notice the tremor in the banker's hands. Who could blame him? Macalester thought. He'd hate like hell to have to try to sell anything to this crowd, after that spiel.

Jefferson cleared his throat, and his voice shook uncontrollably.

"What's the matter, Jefferson, you nervous?" The remark was greeted with laughter, remarkable for its mirthlessness. The crowd was not in a joking mood.

"Unh, the first . . . unh . . . We have a tractor over here, you've all had a chance to inspect it the last three days. It's, unh . . . I think three years old, but in very good shape. Who . . . who wants to open the bidding?"

Jefferson looked imploringly at the crowd. No one said a word. "It's a very good tractor. Matt, unh . . . Mr. Winslow always took good care of his equipment. You all know that."

"Why don't you buy it yourself, Jefferson? Try some honest work for a change." Hoots and catcalls scattered through the crowd. Jefferson buried his nose in the clipboard.

One by one Jefferson sought bids on the items on his checklist. One by one his offers were spurned. As each item was offered, the silence became more hostile. Toward the end of his checklist, Jefferson didn't even bother to wait for the silence. He rushed from item to item. Finally he looked at the crowd in desperation.

"Look, you've all seen what's available here. Is there anything anybody cares to bid on?"

"I like your suit, Jefferson," the big stranger hollered. "How much you want for them pinstripes?"

While the laughter subsided, Akins moved to the rear of the podium. He climbed up the steps and stood beside the harried banker. Leaning in front of Jefferson, he shushed the crowd.

"All right, I think we made our point. How about it?"

The roar was deafening.

"But that doesn't solve Matt Winslow's problem. Now, I've done a little checking, had a talk with Matt a few days ago. I happen to know he owns Downing Savings and Loan $31,259. And forty-two cents. That's a lot of money. But farming is a big job, and a tough one. The times are even tougher. We can't let men like Matt Winslow be driven off their land. So . . . I have here a cashier's check in that very amount, and as it happens, it's made out to Downing Savings and Loan. I also have Matt Winslow's copy of his mortgage."

Akins reached into his hip pocket and tugged a thick sheaf of paper free, waving it over his head. "We all know who the enemy is, and God knows it don't make much sense to me to give him what he wants. But sometimes you have to do what's best, even if it ain't what's right."

Akins handed the check to Jefferson, who, in his anxiety, dropped it. Holding the mortgage high over his head, Akins reached into his shirt pocket. He pulled out a glittering metal box. "You all have seen a Zippo before. I'm going to show you why it was invented."

He thumbed the wheel, and a pale hole appeared above the wick, the lighter's flame invisible under the harsh sunlight. With a flourish he brought the flame to the edge of the mortgage, waited for it catch, then closed the lighter. Akins fanned the air with the flaming papers.

"And the last part of our message to the federal government, without whom the bankers couldn't bleed us dry, is this: Mortgages ain't the only things that burn."

CHAPTER 5

Ferris, Arkansas, couldn't have been any sleepier. Swaggart Avenue, the broad, tree-lined main street named for the town's first mayor, was nine blocks long. The heart of town, four blocks square, was unremarkable. A central square, monitored by the obligatory statue of Stonewall Jackson, horse arear, featured four cobbled walks meeting at a circular plaza.

The beds of marigolds lining each walkway were in full bloom. Recent heat had withered the leaves a little, but notice had been taken. Tomorrow morning, first thing, a little extra water would be provided, and the morning watering would continue until the heat broke. Mayor Thomas Mitchell would see to it, and since the First National Bank of Ferris, of which Mitchell just happened to be director, was footing the bill, it wouldn't cost the town a penny.

Mitchell took his jobs, both of them, seriously. The title of mayor, largely ceremonial when he'd been elected to his first term, had come to mean something. Now, six months into his third consecutive term, it meant more work than he had bargained for. But he had asked for it, and having gotten what he wanted, he was not about to complain. It was unseemly, perhaps the strongest condemnation of which he was capable.

Pulling back the thick gauze of the front drapery, Mitchell

pressed his nose against the gold lettering of the bank's front window. The letters blurred off into incomprehensibility on either side of his flattened nose. The town square, just across the street, was a mass of shadows writhing with the half-hearted zeal of lethargic snakes. It was too damn hot to work, even with the air conditioner on, and since he had never cared for the artificial feel of conditioned air, he preferred to work with his office window open. The thick, dust-filled air was too heavy even for the town's most energetic man.

The footsteps behind him tapped softly. Without turning around he said, "Too hot downstairs, Bill?"

"Yes, sir, Mr. Mitchell. I'm surprised you're still here. I'm supposed to work the night shift, but you ought to be home."

"Too restless, Bill. I haven't slept too much since Martha passed."

"I know how that is. You were as close as any two people I ever saw. Must be a trial for you."

"I'd like to say I'll get used to it, Bill, but I swear to God, I don't think I ever will. The bank and the town are all I got. No kids, and with Martha gone, I don't know . . . maybe I can work myself to sleep."

"Work yourself to death, more likely."

"Feel like some checkers, Bill?"

"Yes, sir, Mr. Mitchell. I'll set 'em up."

"All right, and open a couple of beers, will you? I'll finish up in my office and see you downstairs in a few minutes. It's got to be cooler down there."

"Not so's you'd notice."

Mitchell finally turned away from the window. The elderly guard was already halfway across the polished marble floor on his way to the service elevator. Since Mitchell's wife had died the preceding summer, the old man was about his only company. They weren't friends, exactly; Bill McCallum was too aware of the difference in their status for that to be possible. But they met in some neutral zone as equals, as two lonely men, their best years behind them, both of them with a passion for checkers.

Mitchell walked to the elevator, pressed the button, then

turned around to survey the main lobby while he waited for Bill McCallum to send the self-service car up. The lobby, like the rest of the bank and, most importantly, like its books, was neat and in good order. In a way, he realized, he was fortunate to have something so demanding as the bank to throw into the insatiable void left in his life by his wife's death. He wondered what others, with less demanding work to do, or none at all, did to fill the interminable hours from sunrise to sunrise.

The elevator car whisked to a halt, and he turned just as the door slid open. Inside, he noticed the sharp scent of lemon oil and absently ran his fingertips over the dark wood paneling. The smooth wood felt warm and solid to his touch. He raised his now scented fingers to his nose and inhaled deeply.

The elevator lurched to a halt and he pressed the "Door open" button. Stepping into the narrow, dimly lit corridor, he noticed that, as he had suspected, it was several degrees cooler. Mitchell was halfway down the corridor when the blast roared through like a runaway freight train. He fell to the hard floor, turning to one side and landing on his right shoulder. A sharp pain lanced across his back, and the arm went limp.

Smoke billowed in a thick gray cloud, swirling down the stone-walled corridor like a flash flood in an arroyo. He could just barely make out the figure of Bill McCallum stepping into the hallway.

"Mr. Mitchell? Mr. Mitchell, you all right? What the hell happened?"

Mitchell struggled to rise, but his one good arm was too shaky to support his weight. McCallum, bending low to avoid the worst of the smoke, raced toward him. He realized the blast must have come from behind him. He hauled himself to a seated posture and turned toward the far end of the hall. He wondered what could have caused the explosion. It couldn't have been gas, or he would have smelled it.

Then it hit him. The alarm hadn't sounded. But why? Before he had a chance to consider possible explanations, he spotted a shadowy movement, mostly obscured by the still rolling smoke. Almost at the same instant he felt McCallum's hands under his arms.

"Let me help you, Mr. Mitchell. We got to get out of here."

"Who's there?" Mitchell called, ignoring McCallum's offer and shrugging free of the old man's grip. "Who's there?"

The shadows froze, and Mitchell knew it hadn't been his imagination. Someone was standing there. He couldn't see what they looked like or how many of them there were. He knew only that there were more than one and that they were responsible for the explosion.

"Bill," Mitchell whispered, "you got another gun?"

He clamped his hand over the old man's mouth. McCallum nodded yes.

"All right, leave me your gun and go get the other one. quick!"

Mitchell heard the old man scurry down the hall, choking and wheezing in the smoke-clotted air. The shadows at the opposite end grew agitated. They seemed more substantial as the smoke began to thin out. Mitchell called again.

"Who's there?"

Angry whispers grated on the walls, but Mitchell couldn't make any sense of them. One shadow detached itself from the others and moved toward him. He realized that they couldn't see him any better than he could see them. That was about to change. Mitchell started to drag himself backward with his good arm, pressing himself against the wall. Plaster dust and concrete fragments grated under him as he moved.

It was only then that he understood what was happening. And if these intruders wanted to blow the bank, they would probably not shrink from killing him and McCallum. The shadow advanced cautiously. The air was cleaner toward the ceiling as the heavier dust settled to the floor. A shapeless head and shoulders loomed out of the smoke. Mitchell raised McCallum's pistol and pointed it in the general direction of the figure.

"Stop right there. I have a gun."

The figure stopped. The head turned away, then back. The first burst of gunfire, strangely muted, cracked in the narrow hall. A tight circle of fire had slammed into his chest and neck. He sprawled backward, conscious only of the warm, sticky feeling inside his shirt. The shadow sprinted toward him, towering over him in the swirling, opaque air. Mitchell reached out with his good arm and closed his fingers around a heavy boot. His fingers groped upward, past straps and stiff laces, and grabbed desperately at a ballooning pant leg.

Something pressed against his forehead. It was hot and cold. And so heavy. Mitchell thought of McCallum and the checker game.

Then he died.

Bill McCallum heard the gunfire. He scrambled in the bottom drawer of his desk, looking for his second gun. His fingers seemed stiff, and he kept losing his grip on the accumulated junk of twenty-five years in the basement.

Finally he found it. He hefted the heavy colt .45 automatic, a relic of his military service, thumbed the safety off, and checked the action in instinctive regression. He didn't bother to see if it was loaded. He didn't have to. It always was. That, too, had stayed with him since Inchon, in Korea.

He tiptoed toward the open door, wondering what he was up against. The gunfire had been an automatic weapon, that much was certain, but it had been suppressed. And Mr. Mitchell hadn't returned fire. That, too, was certain. He didn't want to think about what that might mean, knowing full well it didn't matter what he thought. If they had killed Mr. Mitchell, they would certainly kill him, unless he got them first.

He peered out into the hallway. It was still thickly choked with smoke and dust, most of the debris blown his way by the force of the explosion. The control panel for the basement lighting was behind him on the wall. He stepped back, opened the metal door, and leaned in to read the labels. Finding the one he wanted, he yanked it, and the dull glow in the hallway vanished, replaced by the dim, hellishly red haze of the two emergency lamps.

He moved back to the doorway, keeping flat to the wall. He was about to step out and drop to the floor, where the air was thicker, when a blocky shadow materialized in the doorway. It was outlined by a stark red halo. A bright sword slashed out from a flashlight and began slicing back and forth across the small room.

Bill McCallum raised the Colt and squeezed. The gun bucked, and the figure fell backward with a grunt. The heavy pistol sounded thunderous after the deadly whisper of the intruder's weapon. He'd hit the mark but barely. His perspective was off, and his angle of fire bad. Wounded, maybe out of action, the fallen man groaned in the hallway. Footsteps— two men, maybe three—raced down the hall.

"In there." The voice was sibilant, hissing through teeth clenched against pain.

Two more spears of light lanced into the darkened room. Bill cringed into the corner, taking what cover he could behind a folding chair. One of the lights found him. He fired blindly, emptying the magazine. The bright light never wavered. The first hiss of return fire shredded the molded metal back of the chair, adding its small knives to the dozen rounds perforating the old guard from crotch to balding head. He was dead before he tumbled to one side and hit the floor with a barely audible thud, more appropriate to a sack of damp grain than an old man who loved to play checkers.

"All right, let's blow the vault and get the hell out of here."

"I thought you said there'd be nobody here."

"Well, now there ain't." The taller of the two shadows laughed, slinging his rifle over his shoulder. "Let's patch up the asshole and get to work."

CHAPTER 6

Luke Simpson paced restlessly. The terrace overlooking the desert was usually a place where he could piece together a puzzle. The deep blue sky, seemingly endless, covered him like a clear blue bubble of impenetrable silence. Even Jake O'Bannion, the irrepressible executive administrator of Deadly Force, Inc., wouldn't disturb him out there. Jake, who knew only as much about good manners as most New Yorkers, took regulations as challenges, but the sight of Luke pacing, hands folded behind his back, one eye cocked on the cloudless expanse above him, was enough to stop even the bullheaded former cop.

Jake had the run of the place, and certainly Luke was no tyrant, so his job wouldn't be in jeopardy. But O'Bannion had the healthy respect for melancholy that seemed the deepest vein in the Irish personality, mingling inextricably with all the other contrary strands of passion and reason that made the Irish so infuriatingly unpredictable, no matter how many times removed from the old sod. And Jake was only second-generation.

Tracing stolen munitions was not usually an easy job, because those adept enough to pull it off—and from a military installation, to boot—were usually careful enough to cover their tracks pretty well. Luke personally had been involved in two similar investigations, one dating back to his days in San Perplejo when his SWAT team had gone toe-to-toe with a self-styled "Liberation Army" of the Symbionese variety. And those bastards had taken the guns to use. They went through most of the pirated ammo in less than two weeks, burning it up with all the zeal of a merchant seaman going through six months of paychecks.

But that had been another time. Amateurs made amateurish mistakes. And most home-grown radical groups, at least those without some serious counsel from the KGB or Libyan advisers, lasted a couple of weeks at best. To them guns were toys, the kind of thing you bought at K-Mart after a movie and lost interest in after the fifth wave of Red Chinese or Viet Cong swept across the vacant lot and died bloodlessly by the bushel. The muddy excavation, too big for a foxhole, made your pants wet, and you went home, then came out with a glove and ball to get down to some serious play.

But things had begun to change. Foreign advice was getting easier to come by, and the soft underbelly of America, vulnerable to anyone with a genuine desire to wreak havoc, was getting to be too tempting for terrorists of any and all persuasions, and either end of the political spectrum, to ignore. So it was logical to look to the foreign connection as the most likely explanations for the missing weapons.

What puzzled Luke more than any other aspect of the mystery, however, was the ease with which it had been pulled off. Inside information was certainly a real possibility, but Luke was beginning to think it might have gone even deeper than that. Outright assistance to the thieves seemed almost indisputable. That left motive.

If someone in the military, knowledgeable enough and with enough clout to secure and credibly fake the orders that got the hijackers inside the armory, were involved, the dimensions of the problem could be far larger than anyone had suspected. It was not beyond the realm of possibility that some mole, having wormed his way up through the ranks, was now beginning to turn the system against itself, using America's own machinery against it. And if that were true, not only was the problem more complicated, but also it was more deadly. Colonel Milford seemed to have hinted at the possibility without really spelling it out.

Looking out at the seamless fabric of sand and saguaro, Luke thought it an apt metaphor for the problem confronting him. Every place he had looked so far, he had come up empty. If there was a loose end in the cloth, something he could grab on to and pull to unravel the whole thing, he had yet to find it. Even the Arab master weavers, who executed the most intricate imaginable designs in their priceless carpets, deliberately left a flaw, artfully concealed but no less real, because only Allah was without imperfection. If the architects of this little operation were less humble, Luke was certainly going to have his hands full.

He looked at the distant purple blur of the mountains, beginning to darken into its nighttime hue, then turned abruptly and walked to the sliding glass door to the terrace. He pushed it open, stepped into the semidarkness of the air-conditioned office, and pulled the glass shut behind him.

The papers on his desk were as neatly stacked as he had left them. And they were just as baffling as they had been. He scanned the list of stolen inventory again, as if it were the opening he needed, trying to pry it open without a key. The tally read like a shopping list assembled by a thoughtful chef. There was no excess baggage, no ammo for guns not taken, no guns without ammo. The armor-piercing shells were accompanied by the appropriate weapons, the array of grenades wisely and intelligently chosen. They were complemented by grenade launchers. Whoever had assembled the list was no amateur. He had known what he wanted, and presumably knew exactly what he would be doing with it. And that was the most frightening thing of all.

Luke glanced at the clock on the wall. Ben Sanchez was scheduled to call in in less than an hour. Something had to break soon. They were already six days behind the thieves. In its typical, ass-covering, bureaucratic way, Washington had dragged its feet before calling Deadly Force in. The FBI and the Pentagon squabbled over who had jurisdiction. Army intelligence had "lost" some pertinent files. The CIA had "found" them, files it shouldn't have had in the first place, but they had to be "sanitized" before anyone could look at them. All in the name of national security. Milford seemed like a decent guy and, although a little stuffy, unlikely to be any more tolerant of bureaucratic horseshit than Luke himself. And while the bickering and gamesmanship went on, national security went down the tubes, probably now as far underground as the thieves themselves. And all Jake had to do was go down and dig it out.

No problem.

Jake had left the afternoon intel summary in the "in" box. Luke picked it up absently, riffled through it with a thumb, then grunted. He might as well check it out. He sat down heavily, tilting his chair back and reaching up to click on the reading lamp on the wall behind him.

He had more on his plate than some stolen weapons. Maybe he could solve something else. Maybe there was something he could do that wouldn't seem so damn useless. And maybe hell really would freeze over.

By page five, Luke was losing his patience. Something about the armory heist was chewing at him. He leaned farther back in the chair, heard it bump the wall, and closed his eyes. A moment later he heard a knock at the door.

"Come in, it's open." Luke didn't bother to open his eyes.

"Don't you look the very picture of the modern executive! America's mothers will sleep better tonight knowing you're on the job."

"Jake, sometimes your sarcasm really burns my ass."

"Only because it contains a germ of truth, milord."

"You better have a good reason to bust in here."

"Don't I always, now, lad? Don't I always?"

"What is it this time?"

"Did you happen to read that little vignette about the bank robbery in Arkansas? Almost as good as Mickey Spillane, I thought. Wrote it myself."

"You think Spillane is high art."

"Anyone named Mickey is all right in my book, lad."

"What about the bank?"

"I'm not sure. I just think there might be something more than meets the eye."

"You always think that."

"And there usually is, no?"

"Tell me about it. I'm too tired to read. I can't see straight."

"A little draft of the old Jameson's will cure that. Anyhow, it struck a responsive chord in my suspicious New York nature. It seems the bank was only a few hundred miles from the Ozark Armory."

"So what? You draw a few-hundred-mile circle around anyplace, you're liable to find a bank job or two."

"Maybe so, maybe so. But how many of them will be blown open with C-4? How many will show signs of M16 gunfire? And how many will have been perpetrated by banditti shod in government-issue combat boots?"

Luke sat up with a jolt. "Are you joking?"

"No, sir, laddie. I assure you, I'm not joking."

"What kind of lab info can we get?"

"Not much. I already checked. The Ozark Mountain daredevils are less than current in their criminological sophistication."

"Well, what are you standing there for? Get your ass down there. Pull strings. Get Colonel Milford to use his own lab, or the FBI lab. I want access to all the evidence. I want a complete lab work-up, and use the federal club if you need it. I especially want neutron-activation analysis of any projectiles recovered. You know the drill."

"My plane leaves in ninety minutes."

"Jake, you're a good man."

"I know. It's part of me charm."

"Call me as soon as you have anything."

The jump to Ferris by rented car was two hours. Jake, ever conscious of the highway patrol's habit of lurking in blind curves and hiding in dense foliage, kept to the speed limit. It wasn't easy. His foot itched, and he kept watching the Chevy's speedometer with nervous glances. The first hour was a four-lane highway, and he could push it a little, but once he jumped off for the last forty miles, it got tedious.

He had no idea what to expect once he got to Ferris. He'd spoken to the local sheriff on the phone, and the man had seemed cooperative, within limits. Jake knew how jealous of local authority a cop could be. He'd been there himself more than once. And the mention of the FBI was certain to raise hackles. The bureau was notorious for going out of its way to humiliate those who had less glamorous duties and considerably fewer resources.

But without the bureau, Jake wouldn't have had access at all. As it was, it had taken more than a few strings getting pulled to gain entrée to the investigation of what most people were convinced was little more than a bank robbery laced with a double homicide. Truth to tell, Jake himself wasn't sure it was more than that. But the possibility was there, and the precious few leads they'd had were almost exhausted. If there was a link between the bank and the armory, the sooner they learned about it, the better.

As Ferris loomed up through his bug-splattered windshield, Jake threw caution to the winds. He stomped on the gas, letting the Chevy burn off a little carbon. The worst that could happen was, they'd haul him to the sheriff, and since that's exactly who he wanted to see, it might save him some time.

The streets were sunbaked, the asphalt throwing off wavy lines more appropriate to the Arizona desert. Finding the sheriff's office wasn't hard. He pulled into a reserved space, the last of a half dozen angled parking slots alongside the office, and stepped out into a blast furnace. The handle burned his fingers as he slammed the door shut. Checking his watch, he realized he was half an hour early, despite his highway caution.

Inside, a bored deputy, large enough for the front four of the Dallas Cowboys, arrested a pencil in midair to look at him expectantly.

"Sheriff Hodges around?"

"In back. He expecting you?"

"Yeah, name's O'Bannion."

"Oh, yeah. You're here about the bank robbery, ain't you?"

"Yeah."

"Come on back." The deputy indicated a gate in the wooden rail separating the law from the general public. For whose convenience? Jake wondered.

He stepped to the gate, pushing it open with one knee, and the deputy led him to a rear office. Jake stopped for a few seconds in front of a large oscillating fan, letting the waves of hot air wash over him before passing through the doorway into the sheriff's office.

A middle-aged man, the color of light coffee and even larger than the deputy, stood to greet him. "Mr. O'Bannion, Leroy Hodges."

"Sheriff." Jake shook the offered hand, fearful it might cost him a few fingers. "I'm not interrupting anything, am I?"

"No, not at all. I was just going over the files again. The feds aren't even here yet. Not that I'm surprised. We don't see them Hollywood types but once or twice a decade. Have a seat. Can I get you something cold?"

"I don't suppose you'd have a beer handy, would you?"

"Well, now, I'll tell you. I never liked drinking on the job. And as a black man in these parts, I have to use a little extra caution. See, sheriff is an elected office down here."

"I understand. Iced tea'll be fine."

"Be right back." Hodges stood again, and Jake realized just how big the man was. At least 6' 5", maybe more. He crossed the office in two steps, dwarfing the old refrigerator in one corner of the room as he bent to peer inside it.

A moment later he was back, a can in each hand. He slapped them on the scarred desktop, popped the lids, and offered one to Jake, who took a long pull. He almost choked, then tipped his glasses back to read the label.

"How long has Lone Star been making iced tea, Sheriff?"

"Damn, did I give you a beer? That's probably evidence. But since you already opened it, it guess it ain't much good now, is it?" He laughed easily, and Jake relaxed for the first time since leaving Phoenix. Working with Leroy Hodges wasn't going to be half bad.

CHAPTER 7

The forest was impenetrable. The thick canopy overhead, branches interlaced and bound together with tangled vines, dripped heavy Spanish moss. Wiry undergrowth laced with thorns and prickly, razor-edged leaves grabbed at arms and legs. Underfoot, the spongy cushion frequently gave way to standing water, invisible under the clumped grass.

Bugs by the millions, fit for a textbook on insect adaptability, swarmed in the humid shadows. Every step seemed to irritate a thousand mosquitoes. Just ahead, a fetid stream, its water dark with decaying vegetation, moved sluggishly through the near jungle. Off to the left, a raised hummock, sprouting a few sumac trees and little else, looked like an island to a shipwrecked sailor. Wilson Fontenot hacked at the last dozen yards of undergrowth, his machete loosely held in one blistered hand.

He struggled up the raised side of the hummock, thorn-laden vine snagging repeatedly around his tired ankles. Finally, above the swamp for the first time in three hours, he fell heavily, facedown. Even the stiff spikes of grass stabbing at his cheeks seemed welcome. He lay quietly for several minutes, listening to the forest stretching off in every direction, as far as he could see. The stand of trees around the hummock was relatively thin. Overhead, the noontime sun beat down on his broad back, simultaneously drying his muck-soaked fatigue pants and raising a sweat between his shoulder blades.

When he had heard nothing after several minutes of intense concentration, he rolled over onto his back, stretching his legs full-length to let them dangle off the edge of the hummock. An intense pain shot through his right calf, and he sat up, tearing at the blousy pant leg. He rolled it up past his knee and twisted the leg to one side. He spotted the leech immediately. Nearly three inches long, it had latched on to the calf. A small circle of blood oozed out from around the slimy parasite. With a curse, Fontenot grasped the slippery thing between thumb and forefinger, losing his grip twice before wrenching it loose. In frustration, he squeezed the leech tightly, and it burst like a small sausage. Fontenot nearly gagged, then wiped the ruptured leech and a generous amount of his own blood on the rough grass beside him.

This was no picnic. And he was rapidly losing his patience. He'd already started grumbling in the barracks, but no one seemed to share his discontent. And more than one of his bunk mates had warned him to keep his opinions to himself. Like nearly every other group Fontenot had ever joined, it seemed like the Heartlanders were going to be easier to get into than out of. Even Parris Island hadn't been this hot, and the discipline was almost as rough. The Marine Corps was starting to seem like paradise compared to the primitive life at the camp.

Fontenot yanked his canteen free and shook it. The hollow sound of the sloshing water wasn't encouraging. At best, he had a cup or so left, and it was bound to be about as refreshing as warm spit. His mouth was dry, and his lips were beginning to crack from the intense sun. Judging by the sun, it was still early, two-thirty or three at the latest. That meant four more hours of slogging around in the swamp.

He was glad he hadn't been eliminated but was no longer sure that winning was worth the price he had to pay. Hell, a weekend off was his right. Even the sawmill gave him that.

But then, he no longer had a job at the sawmill—or anyplace else, for that matter.

Fontenot unscrewed the cap and filled his mouth with the warm water. He swirled it around a few times, then spit it over the edge of the hummock. The salty taste was gone, and the broken bits of bug and the dry pods of a dozen seeds had been rinsed away. He filled his mouth a second time, this time letting the water sit a few seconds before swallowing it in a single gulp.

He was screwing the lid back on when he heard the noise. He cocked an ear in the general direction of the sound and listened. He heard nothing but the buzz of insects and the faintest whisper of wind among the treetops. Slipping the canteen back into its webbing, he left the flap open and reached for his rifle.

He hefted the gun cautiously, getting to his knees at the same time. Fontenot hunched closer to the few scraggly trees on the hummock. Wriggling in among the slender trunks, he kept his eyes on that part of the woods where the sound had originated. So far it hadn't been repeated. He was used to being alone in the forest, but as often as he'd been hunting, and through four years in the Marine Corps, he had never lost the shivers that raced along his spine at the first unexpected sound. There was no mistake about it . . . someone was out there.

Fontenot dropped to his stomach, careful not to move the trees that offered him his only cover. They wouldn't protect him very well, and they could just as easily betray his presence, but they were all he had. Lying flat on the stiff grass, he scanned the woods, looking for something, anything, that didn't belong.

In the distance he heard the shrill whistle of a bird. It sounded genuine, but you could never be too sure. The call was repeated, this time closer, and Fontenot tensed in expectation. He eased the M16 forward, making sure he could swing the muzzle in a wide arc without snagging on the thin trunks concealing him. He reached out with his left hand to sweep away some dead leaves, then froze. The cold shivers returned. He closed his eyes, took a deep breath, and held it.

When it was no longer possible to contain himself, he expelled the air slowly, the way his grandfather used to exhale the last drag of his last cigarette of the day. There was then, as now, something final in the gesture, as if the breath might well be his last.

The cottonmouth was still there, its coils looser, as if it were preparing to move. If it had seen him, it made no sign. Slowly, his lower lip clenched between his teeth, he pulled back the hand. It trembled violently, but any sudden move would invite the water moccasin to strike. The blades of grass seemed to rattle like sabers, their rasping shudder sending echoes out across the swampy forest floor. Then, with supreme indifference, the snake raised its head and stared him in the eye for a second. Its movement caused the faintest hiss as it slithered over the dry grass. Then it was gone.

Fontenot let out a great sigh and climbed to his knees. He was still shaking.

"Your troubles ain't over, cowboy."

Fontenot started to turn, but the sharp prod between his shoulder blades discouraged his curiosity.

The report of the rifle echoed through the forest, and Fontenot was aware of the acrid bite of coordinate. He almost didn't notice the sharp slap of the projectile on his left shoulder. Only then did he feel the sticky ooze trickling down his spine.

Dyed red, Wilson Fontenot wouldn't win this one.

He started to turn, but a sharp blow from a rifle butt caught him just over the left ear. He lay on his back, not quite sure why, for a second, staring up at the unblinking sun. Then it got dark.

"Stupid son of a bitch, ain't he?"

"Hell, he did all right. He made the cut."

"Akins must be hard up if this turkey made the first team."

"Come on, just tag him and let's get moving in. I don't want to spend the whole damn day out here. The bugs are driving me nuts."

One of the men dropped to one knee. He reached into his pocket for an aerosol can of aluminum paint. With a grand flourish he sprayed a glittering "16" in foot-high numerals in the center of Fontenot's back. He shook the can roughly, retraced the numbers with a sputtering mist of the metallic paint, then tossed the empty container into the weeds.

"All right, let's move out. We got fifteen more out there. We don't get 'em all by sundown, Akins'll shit a brick."

"Fuck Akins. I don't see him humping it out here. Too damn high-and-mighty for the dirty work."

"Man signs your paycheck, he can damn well tell you to walk on your hands, he wants to."

"You, maybe."

"You, too, Andy. I don't see you give him no back talk. You run your mouth pretty good when he ain't around to hear you."

"He ain't around much, these days."

"Man got to get the cash. He can't do that sittin' on no bunk in this shithole."

"You ask me, he's more interested in getting his picture took. Them shades he wears, you'd think he was a goddamn movie star."

"Jealous?"

"Not really. But he could pay a little better."

"There's more important things to do with the money."

The two men disappeared in the forest, still arguing. They were gone no more than five minutes when Fontenot groaned. He shook his head, then placed a finger gingerly on his left temple. He gasped and yanked the fingers away. The pain felt like somebody had driven a white-hot needle into his scalp. He glanced at the fingers casually, then wiped the watery smear of blood on his fatigues. The knot on his scalp was the size of a hen's egg. He cursed his unseen assailants, rolled over, then tried to sit up.

The pain lanced through his head again, and he fell back with a moan. Things were supposed to be serious, but not for real. The blow on his head could have killed him. He wondered whether his attackers knew, or even cared, whether he was still alive. Carrying instruction to the limit, they had nearly cracked his head open. His back felt sticky, and he thought for a second he might be bleeding from another wound, this one in the back.

He tried again to sit, reaching behind him with wary fingers. He grabbed a sticky clump of his shirt, then looked at his fingers. Instead of the red he expected, he noticed the gleaming silver smear. Curious, he shucked off the shirt and twirled it around to read the still wet inscription.

The ''16'' meant nothing to him. Was it a signature of some kind? He racked his brain, the effort renewing the shooting pains in his head. Then it dawned on him, slowly. Somebody was stalking all of them, taking them out one by one and, like a biologist doing fieldwork, tagging them. He'd seen Marlin Perkins on television, *Zoo Parade* or something like that, tag everything from alligators to zebras. But Marlin Perkins was a little easier on his quarry. He never left a lump the size of a golf ball on any of his victims.

Now, if only he knew what the ''16'' meant. Did it mean he was the sixteenth one nailed? He hoped not. There were more than seventy guys participating in the exercise. If he were the sixteenth one zapped, that meant over fifty-four guys were still out there. A TV show ranked fifty-fourth didn't have much of a future. His own wouldn't be much brighter.

Fontenot was still groggy. He shook his head, wincing from the pain, then got to his knees. Whatever else was happening, he knew, sure as hell, that he was finished for the day. No way in hell he was going to spend one more minute than he had to in the godforsaken swamp. Using the nearest tree as a crutch, he hauled himself painfully to his feet.

Checking his watch, he realized he had been out less than fifteen minutes. Judging by the sun, the camp would be directly behind him. There was no telling how far away it was. One of the rules of the exercise was that there be no maps. The whole point, Akins had insisted, was to see just how good you were. When push came to shove, you had nobody but yourself to depend on. Teamwork was the primary goal, but for teamwork to be possible, each man had to feel that every other member of the team was as competent as he was. Nobody worth his salt would put his life in the hands of an asshole. Consequently each man had to prove, to the satisfaction of all the others, that he wasn't an asshole. Then, and only then, would he be welcomed to the club.

Recruits were a dime a dozen. Those with the goods were few and far between. Wilson Fontenot wasn't sure what was happening, but he sure as shit felt like an asshole.

CHAPTER 8

Leroy Hodges stretched his enormous frame, raising his hands high over his head. Jake noticed that the sheriff's fingertips scraped the ceiling.

"How about a little lunch, Southern-style, Mr. O'Bannion?"

"Sounds good to me, Sheriff."

"Leroy, call me Leroy. 'Sheriff' is for people who have to see me every day." The big man laughed easily.

Jake was impressed with the man. And he was hungry. A chance to sit down someplace quiet would be welcome. Years in the sinkhole of the New York crime world had taught him that sometimes people know more than they're willing to divulge while sitting in the stiff formality of an office. That was just as true of law officers as it was of private citizens. And almost since he'd arrived, Jake had the suspicion Leroy Hodges had something on his mind. But off-the-record.

"You like soul food, Jake?"

"Some. Ribs and chicken, yeah. Collard greens, you can have."

"How about bean pie?"

"Now that I like. I used to go up to Harlem all the time, after the Muslims got going. They made a bean pie that was out of this world. Shazam, or Shabazz or something, it was

53

called. There weren't too many places carried it, but it was worth the trip.''

"Then wait'll you try the bean pie at Bertha's. A place outside of town, about five miles. It's worth the trip too.''

"Let's go." Jake got up sluggishly, still drained from his trip.

The sheriff left his hat on the desk. As they stepped out into the afternoon sun, now at full boil, he snapped a pair of mirrored sunglasses from his shirt pocket. "Usually wear these to ticket strangers. Makes him feel they really been down South." He laughed. "Normally I can't stand the damn things. Let's take your car."

Jake glanced sideways at the big man. If Hodges didn't want to use his own car, chances were he didn't care to advertise his lunch with the man from out of town. Jake's pulse rate went up a few beats.

Jake opened the rented car and slid in to crank it up and turn on the air-conditioning, then he backed out again. "It's a damn oven in there. Let's let it cool off bit."

"Hell, man, you from Arizona. This shouldn't bother you. Let's go." Hodges ducked quickly into the car, slamming the door loudly behind him.

Jake shrugged and dropped into the driver's seat. Hodges gave him directions, and they were outside town in a matter of minutes. Hodges opened a fresh pack of Marlboros and thumbed a battered Zippo into life. He took a long drag on the cigarette, then stared reflectively at its glowing tip.

They drove in silence, the outlying buildings growing farther and farther apart. Small farms, their barns and silos emblems of hard times, sat back away from the road on either side, paint peeling in quiet desperation.

"Slow up a minute, Jake. Look at that."

Jake followed the pointing finger to a battered tractor, red as much from rust as from paint. Tall weeds sprouted through the spokes of its ancient wheels. "Looks like an antique," Jake said.

"It is. But the damn thing was plowing fields last fall. It's hard times, Jake. Real hard times."

"I been reading about it."

"Ain't the same thing. People around here, they're under the gun. They're so hard-pressed, they don't even care what color I am."

"I never thought of Arkansas as Deep South, anyway, Sheriff. I'm not too surprised."

"That's 'cause you don't remember Orville Faubus, our esteemed governor a few years back. Ross Barnett and George Wallace used him as a role model. Hell, man, school desegregation started right here in Arkansas. And it's Leroy, I already told you."

"Something on your mind, Leroy?"

"In due time, Jake. I'll get to it. First we got to get some grease. Hang a left."

Jake skidded on loose gravel as he made the sudden turn. The road was rutted, its shoulder a narrow strip of weeds between rock and ditch.

"On the right, over there."

Jake spotted a hand-lettered sign, its blue paint bleached to a pale gray by years of harsh sunlight. BERTHA'S KITCHEN, it read. The building itself was little more than a shack. Its dusty windows sported gingham curtains almost as old as Jake.

"Doesn't look like much."

"You want to look, go to a museum. You want to eat, no place better than Bertha's that I know of."

The car skidded on loose gravel and sand in the makeshift parking lot. Jake killed the engine, then sat with both hands on the steering wheel.

"Don't just sit there, man. Come on."

Jake nodded. He slipped out from behind the wheel and started after the sheriff. "Hang on a second, Leroy." He walked back and opened the car to remove the keys.

"Hell, you could have left them. They won't be any safer in your pocket." Hodges grinned. "Folks around here are honest."

"Tell that to Mayor Thomas Mitchell, Leroy."

The sheriff's face clouded over. "I'll get to that inside."

Jake followed the big man into the shack. The sheriff had to bend to avoid rapping his head on the low lintel. It was dark inside, and Jake blinked to adjust his eyes. He was still struggling with the dim light when a voice hollered, "My, my, Leroy Hodges. You *must* be hungry. Man your size needs a good meal ever'day."

As the gloom lifted, Jake spotted a slender young black woman coming toward them. She was drying her hands on a well-used apron. She stood on tiptoe to peck at Hodges's chin. She was thirty years younger, and fifty pounds lighter, than Jake had been expecting. Her coffee-colored skin was smooth and tight. Generous breasts struggled with the faded blue of a neatly starched, pressed work shirt. Long legs would have given the impression of height if she hadn't been dwarfed by the sheriff. She might have been the most beautiful woman Jake had ever seen. He wasn't sure she wasn't.

She stepped back, hands on hips to look at the two of them. Her almond-shaped eyes, even in the dim light, sparkled with good humor. "You want the usual table?"

"What else?"

"Well, it's yours. As soon as you introduce me to your friend. Where's your manners?"

"I was coming to that. Jake O'Bannion, Samantha Tyler."

"Samantha?" Jake raised an eyebrow.

The young woman laughed. "Would you eat at a place called 'Samantha's'?"

"Only to watch yuppies in their native habitat."

Samantha laughed again, a musical trill with a smoky undercurrent. Her contralto voice sounded as good as she looked. "Bertha was my grandma. She founded the place, if so exalted a word is possible in this connection. I took it over when I got tired of teaching."

"What'd you teach?"

"Political science. University of Chicago."

"I'm impressed," Jake said.

"And not just by your education, I'm guessing." Hodges poked Jake in the ribs. "Come on, let's eat. Samantha, if you got a few minutes, I'd like you to sit in on things a little later."

Samantha looked puzzled but nodded her agreement. "Whatever you say, Leroy." She led them to a small, neat table in one corner. It was set for two, and a pair of menus stood on end between ketchup and sugar.

"I'll be back for your order in a few minutes."

When she was gone, Jake turned to Hodges. "What's going on? I have the distinct impression I'm in a play without having seen the script."

"Maybe you are, Jake. But, hell, all you Micks are natural actors."

"Maybe, but we ain't got rhythm."

"Look, I got a few things I want to talk about. As far off-the-record as you can get. I brought you here because it's about the only place I know of where we can do that."

"Have anything to do with the bank robbery?"

"Probably. I can't be sure. But, yeah, I think so."

"All right, then, let's get on with it."

"You trust me to order for you?"

"Why not?"

Hodges stood up and disappeared into the kitchen. He was back a minute later, two beers in one hand, both open, two glasses in the other. He poured both and shoved one across the table to Jake, then sat down.

"I think I know why you're here." Jake opened his mouth, but Hodges held up a finger. "Let me finish. You're not just looking into a bank robbery in some hick town. And that's good, because that isn't what happened to Tom Mitchell."

"What did happen?"

"I'm not sure, but I hear things."

"What kind of things?"

"All kinds. But to begin with, the weapons used on Mitchell and McCallum weren't your standard equipment for a bank job. Neither was the C-4 they used to blow the wall out. Not around here, anyhow."

"How do you know what did it? I thought the lab work wasn't finished."

"Six years in Special Forces teach you a lot. I know a demo job when I see it, and I know what an M16 does to a wall, not to mention an old man or two."

"So?"

"There's more. I hear things. You know, the South is full

of good old boys who were in the Army, are in the Army, or are gonna be in the Army, soon as they get their growth. It's harder to keep a secret than anybody realizes."

"What secret is that?"

"I have a good idea where the guns and C-4 came from. Can't prove it yet, maybe never will. But I know it, sure as I'm sitting here."

"Go on." Jake took a healthy pull on his beer and leaned forward.

"You know about that armory raid, over at Ozark. I heard you on the phone. That means you think there's a connection. And so do I. I don't know what it is, but I know it's there. I also know the men who pulled off the armory thing had some help. Big help."

"How big?"

"We're talking bird colonel, at least. Maybe even bigger. I been reading the papers and watching the wires. But what I hear around tells me a lot more than either one. And what I hear is that somebody on the inside cut the paperwork and supplied a detailed layout of the warehouse. That's why it didn't take any time at all to work out of there with enough shit to keep a small army going for months."

Jake ran nervous fingers through his mop of dark hair. "You got any hard information?"

"Nope! But I got Samantha. Let me get her out here."

The sheriff stood up again, seeming even larger. He vanished into the kitchen again, returning with Samantha Tyler in tow. Hodges yanked a chair from an adjacent table.

"Tell Jake what you told me."

Samantha looked uncertainly at Jake, then at Hodges.

"Go on, tell him. He's on our side."

"You sure?"

"I wouldn't have brought him here if I wasn't. You know that."

"Where do I start "

"The armory . . ." Hodges paused. "Start with the armory."

Samantha took a deep breath. "I told you I used to teach political silence. Old habits die hard. So . . . I sort of use my new life as a research lab, watch people, trends, that sort of thing. A friend of my brother's is stationed at Ozark. He told William—that's my brother—some things that don't make sense, unless . . .''

Jake, absorbed Samantha's story, forgot all about his beer. When she finished, he didn't say anything for a long moment.

"What do you think, Jake?" Hodges asked.

"I don't know. I mean, it makes sense, of some crazy kind. But I need more than that. I have to have a place to start. Something I can hang the theory on."

"Try Ralston's," Samantha suggested.

"Ralston's?"

"Yeah. It's a bar where the good old boys hang out. Lots of drinking, loose talk, hard-assed bullshit. Redneck heaven. If there's anything to it, you might get the hook you need right there." Hodges paused to finish his beer. "For obvious reasons, I can't go myself."

"What about sending one of your deputies?"

"The thing is, they're my deputies as much because they need a job as anything else. And at least one of 'em is there to keep an eye on me. I can't trust 'em with a thing like this."

"Then how the hell am I likely to get anywhere? I'm a complete stranger."

"True. But you're white." Samantha did not sound apologetic for the observation. "The kind of men we're talking about, that's all that really matters. Unless you're also Jewish. Are you?"

"Rabbi O'Bannion. I kind of like that." Nobody laughed. Not even Jake.

CHAPTER 9

Jake heard Ralston's Bar two blocks before he saw the garish neon sign announcing its presence. Three blocks off the main drag, it sat in a long block of stores and offices, all of which did a quieter business, confined to daylight hours. Jake wondered whether Ralston's had chosen the location for that reason, or if any other kind of business had been driven out by the racket.

He had to park nearly a block away. The street's ample parking was largely occupied by pickups and 4×4s, most featuring some variation of the Confederate flag on decals, bumper stickers, fender pennants, or all three. Samantha Tyler has warned him what to expect, but she hadn't prepared him for this. It looked like *some* fun.

The loud music sounded like nothing Jake had ever heard. The country-and-western bars in Arizona were, by and large, rather tame affairs, especially around Phoenix, which had its pretentions to being a major metropolitan area, despite its small-town attitudes. Jake could feel the muscles in his shoulder bunch into hard knots as he reached for the Hollywood double doors and pushed them open, like the new sheriff in a hard-nosed cow town.

The music didn't get any louder once he stepped inside. It

couldn't have. A few couples, mostly in their late twenties and early thirties, tried to maneuver around a tiny dance floor, but for the most part it was a man's bar. Many of the patrons watched the dancers, tilted back with their elbows on the bar, a glass dangling loosely in one hand. The motif was denim and early grit.

A half dozen tables clustered in one end, away from the dance floor. One was empty, and Jake made a beeline for it. He scraped back one of four chairs, its cane bottom well rounded, a few splinters spiking the air. He sat down gingerly. The single waitress, pretty in a hard-faced way and losing a desperate battle to conceal the fact that she was no longer twenty-three, nodded, then waved that she would get his order in a minute.

Jake watched her banter with three men at another table. One of them had an arm draped casually over her hips, his fingers playing with the loose ends of her apron strings. Jake couldn't hear the conversation because of the music, but it was obviously a routine familiar to them all. The waitress leaned over to light a cigarette for a loose-jointed farm boy across the table. The arm-draper stuck something in her cleavage, then said something that made the others laugh. She took a look at it. The flash of green told Jake it was her tip. She said something with a big smile. Whatever it was, it struck home, because the arm-draper looked miffed and the other two laughed.

Finally the band announced a break. Apparently there for the music, the three men stood up to go. Arm-draper bent to kiss the waitress, but she kept her lips out of his reach, and he settled for a loud peck on her cheek. In the newly quiet room, even with his ears still buzzing from the volume, Jake could hear it.

When they were gone, she turned her attention to Jake. Her strut was practiced but still effective. Tight jeans and low-cut blouse called attention away from her face, the only part of her that betrayed her age. She smiled. To Jake, still very much ill at ease so far from home, it seemed genuine. He knew he wanted it to, but there was something real about it, despite the circumstances.

"My name's Jo. I'll be your waitress 'cause I'm the only one this dump has. What'll you have?" She laughed easily, and Jake felt that old stirring.

"Can I get some kind of a sandwich?"

"Sure. Ham, with or without cheese. Hamburger, without or without cheese and/or chili. Steak. Plain. You can have fries or onion rings on the side. Or chili."

"Hell, I don't know. What do you suggest?"

"You want the truth, I suggest you eat before you get here. But since it's too late for that, I'd say have a hamburger. Not too many ways you can ruin one of those, although, God knows, Bobby does his best. A gourmet cook he ain't."

"All right, then. A hamburger and fries, I guess."

"Home or French?"

"French fries. And a beer, whatever's on tap."

"Got it." She tapped the pad with her pencil eraser, then turned sharply, with almost military precision. Jake watched the pendular movement of her hips almost absently. It had been a long time since he'd seen a woman so natural, so at ease with her surroundings. It almost seemed as if she didn't care what anybody thought. She liked herself, and that was good enough.

While Jake was wondering about her, the sound system kicked in. He'd have sworn it was even louder than the band, but it didn't seem scientifically possible. Tammy Wynette started complaining, and Jake tuned out immediately.

Jake watched the farmers at the bar and wondered why they acted like cowboys. Heads turned along the bar, and Jake spotted Jo almost immediately, toting a tray with his burger, fries, and a glass of beer. She carried it lightly, on the tips of up-reaching fingers, using her free arm to fend off hands that grabbed for her as much out of ritual as lust. She was light on her feet, and her thrusts and parries would have made D'Artagnan smile.

At Jake's table, she deftly twirled the tray to its surface, the beer barely rippling in its glass. "You running a tab or you want to pay now?"

"A tab, I guess." Jake smiled. "You must get a few bruises now and then."

She caught the direction of Jake's glance and laughed. "Nope. They haven't laid a hand on me in three years. To tell the truth, I'm not sure they'd know what to do if they got lucky. Sometimes I think about it, just to see what would happen."

"Maybe it's better this way."

"I guess. You want anything else, holler. If the band is playing, stand up and wave a handkerchief."

"I'll want another beer. You might as well bring it whenever you come back this way."

She looked sharply at Jake, made a note on his check, and walked away. Before she disappeared into the crowd, she glanced once more over her shoulder.

Jake bit into the hamburger. He knew immediately what Jo had meant about the cook. The meat was black on the outside and red enough inside to make a cannibal say "Uncle." He tried a couple of fries, and they were better. But not much. Washing the food down with a long gulp of beer, Jake noticed two men who seemed to be as ill at ease as he was. Both wore khaki pants. One had on combat boots, the other city shoes. They stood out enough to make him wonder.

Jake kept an eye on them while he finished his food, eating quickly to avoid tasting it as much as possible. Jo came back with his second beer, plunking it down with a solid crack.

"Anything wrong?" Jake asked.

"No more than usual. This is a bitch of a job. Sometimes it gets to me. I wish . . . never mind. It's nothing personal."

"You sure?"

"Yup."

"I guess I'm not the only stranger tonight, huh?" He nodded toward the khaki pants.

"Oh, them. Yeah, they don't belong here. In more ways than one. Been around for two or three days."

"Listen, do you get a break or do you keep running all night?"

"I'm on my break, why?"

"Buy you a beer "

"Who's gonna bring it to the table?" She laughed.

"I'll go get it."

"All right, but don't get any ideas."

"*Moi?*" Jake feigned innocence, then subverted it with a wink. "Besides, I'm too old for you."

"Not in this bar, you're not. Most of these drugstore cowboys are all talk. I figure you're probably old enough to know how but not old enough to know better."

"I'll be right back. Don't go away." Jake stood and pushed through to the bar, choosing a spot right near the man in the khaki pants. He cocked an ear while he waited for the bartender. The men were talking too softly for him to follow the conversation, but he caught fragments, mostly meaningless. He was about to sidle up closer when the bartender noticed him.

"Beer?" Jake watched the bartender move off, then slid down toward the man in the khaki pants. He caught a few more scraps of conversation, and a name or two, but he wasn't sure whether they referred to people or places. Samantha had told him about the strangers and seemed to think they were somehow significant. She didn't know how but insisted that Jake take a hard look at them. A moment later the beer was delivered. Jake paid and walked back to the table.

Jo thanked him and took a sip as Jake sat down. "You seem pretty interested in those guys. Don't you like women . . . or are you a cop?"

"No, I'm not a cop." Jake wasn't sure she believed him. It was, strictly speaking, the truth, but he felt uncomfortable with the evasive literalness. "As for women, well . . . I'm kind of particular."

"That why you drink with a barmaid you don't even know? Are you *that* particular?"

" 'Don't know' and 'don't want to know' are two different things."

Jo laughed. "Sounds to me like you are getting ideas, even though I warned you about it."

"I *always* have ideas."

"Where you from?"

"Phoenix. I'm here for a few days on business."

"Sure you are. Monkey business, I'll bet."

It was too close to the truth. Jake swallowed uncomfortably. "What about you? What's your story?"

"Story? I don't have a story."

"You're good at your job, but you don't like it very much, do you?"

"What's to like? I wouldn't even be doing it, if it weren't for my husband."

"I didn't realize you were married."

"I'm not. My husband's dead."

"I'm sorry, I didn't know."

"Don't be. He was one of those guys life liked to pick on. When the farm started to go under, I took this job to help with the bills. That was three years ago. It wasn't enough."

"What happened?"

"The bank foreclosed, and Charlie couldn't take it. He turned the tractor loose with a disker behind it. Then he lay down and waited. I heard him scream and I didn't want to look, but there was no way I couldn't. *That's* a sight I'll never forget, if I live to be a hundred." She shuddered, the memory still fresh.

"My God. He must have been desperate to do something like that."

"Desperation? No, that wasn't it. He was too angry, and too tired, to be desperate. I think he figured he'd get even with somebody. Hell, maybe it was me, I just don't know. . . . But it worked. It was better than thumbing his nose, and more insulting than giving us the finger. Kind of a 'fuck you' to all of us. Maybe now it would be different."

"Why do you say that?"

"Because now people seem to care more. About the farmers, I mean."

"Maybe they don't care as much as you think."

"I've thought about that, but a drowning man can't afford to be particular about who throws him the rope."

"No, I suppose not," Jake said. "As long as it *is* a rope."

CHAPTER 10

Tran Cao stared intently at the screen. Ballistics wasn't his thing, but as the principal technical adviser to Deadly Force, he had managed to cultivate a skill, if not a taste. Strictly speaking, what he was engaged in wasn't ballistics at all. Neutron-activation analysis was more like nuclear chemistry. It was not concerned with the flight of projectiles and had very little to do with matching bullets and guns. Rather than visual scrutiny of the physical characteristics of weapons, lands and grooves, unique scars made by imperfections in a gun barrel, this technique was more precise but far more mysterious. It could say, to a certainty, that fragment A was definitely part of projectile B by measuring the metallic composition of both to parts per billion.

Trace elements, and their individual spectrum lines, were as precise as fingerprints, and as indisputable. Deadly Force was still in the process of establishing a lab with the requisite sophistication, but Tran, once assigned to the task by Luke Simpson, had thrown himself into the subject. Now, with the FBI test data in hand, Tran was making sure their conclusions were accurate.

He stared at the screen. One by one he projected film of the distinctive spectrum bands of several hunks of metal on a screen, side by side by side. Each sample had been bombarded with neutrons. Specific trace metals, made radioactive by the bombardment and emitting gamma radiation as a result, were checked. The level of sensitivity was extremely high. There was some noise if too many metals were present, but there was even a way to overcome that. In most cases, however, bullets were composed of relatively few metals and a few trace elements. In this case there was no question about it: The match was perfect. The spectrophotometric comparison was impressively consistent. Turning to the neutron-activation data tape, to get a numerical translation of the visual evidence, he punched a code into the computer and watched the printer expectantly.

A tentative burst from the print head, which came sooner than he'd expected, made him start. As if reading his mind, the printer stopped almost immediately. He wondered whether the giant Cray was sensitive to the enormity of the questions it had been asked, able perhaps to appreciate the life-and-death significance of analytical results. As if second-guessing itself, like a witness who knows what he saw but is bending over backward to be fair, the machine mulled, then started again. Tran grabbed the end of the fanfold paper and held it gently as the machine divulged its conclusions.

When it had finished, Tran form-fed a couple of sheets to tear it off cleanly between two blank pages. He had had too many accidents with printouts ripping in the least acceptable places. It was worth a few extra sheets to make sure the data was received intact. He shut off the printer and left the lab to walk the thirty yards to his office. It was nearly one o'clock in the morning, and his light was the only one burning. He was dimly aware of that fact, but he was used to it, and, truth to tell, preferred it that way. With the yammering of O'Bannion and the kibitzing of Calvin Steeples, he got little done. Science went right out the window whenever either of them walked into the lab. With O'Bannion away and Steeples asleep after his long flight from D.C., ferrying in the test data, Tran could get something done in something close to the amount of time it should reasonably take.

He made a quick photocopy, for annotation, of the printout, then spread the duplicate open on his desk. He dropped into the leather chair, raised several inches to allow for his diminutive stature. He still hadn't gotten used to the enormity of scale that seemed to shape everything in America. By Vietnamese standards, he was average height. By the standards of his adopted country, he was Mickey Rooney with epicanthic folds. That was something about which Steeples never stopped reminding him. One more reason to work the graveyard shift.

Tran made several notes in the margin of his copy. Luke had been right to want the data. The FBI lab had tested all the ammunition batches present in the Ozark Armory. All the stolen cases of M16 ammo had come from a single manufacturing batch. A few cases from the same batch still remained at the warehouse. The test data led to an inescapable conclusion: The bullets that had killed Thomas Mitchell and Bill McCallum had been stolen from the Ozark Armory. There was no way around it.

The conclusion was distressing for more than one reason, but the one that bothered Tran most was this: bullets paid for and manufactured to defend the American people were now being used to kill them. That would have been hard to take in the best circumstances, but when the men who had taken the weapons were using them to rob banks, presumably to get more money to get still more weapons, then it was almost certain things were going to get a hell of a lot worse before they got better.

Luke was hot to catch the thieves, Tran knew. He glanced at the clock over his desk. It was 2:35 A.M. He had finished his annotation. His conclusions were firm and coincided precisely with those of the FBI lab report, a unanimity itself as remarkable as a unicorn. There was no way around it. He would have to wake Luke up.

Tran picked up the phone. He finished dialing, telling himself that if it rang more than four times, he would hang up and risk the boss's fury. It didn't matter. The second ring had barely started when Tran heard Luke on the other end.

"What took you so long?"

"You think nuclear chemistry is a snap?"

"Ballistics always was."

"Ballistics is child's play compared to this technique. It is 'Chopsticks,' and you are measuring it against 'The Art of the Fugue.' "

"Just remember, you mentioned chopsticks, I didn't. Calvin hears about this, you'll never live it down."

"It is so typical of his chauvinism. all Orientals look alike to him. In his judgment I am somehow at fault for the unfinished state of the Great Wall of China, a country I have never even seen."

"Should I come down?"

"I think so."

"See you in five minutes. I'm already dressed. Couldn't sleep."

"I'll see you, then. Bring some coffee."

The black Toyota drifted off the road into a narrow defile among the trees and coasted to a halt. The driver killed the engine. He had been driving without lights for nearly three miles, and his eyes burned from the strain. He opened the door and stepped into the wet weeds.

He closed the door without a sound, pressing it hard until the lock made the slightest click. The dense foliage, augmented by cascades of hanging moss, made the already dark night nearly impenetrable. He squeezed the battery check on a small portable tape recorder, grunted when the small red LED winked at him, and hung the recorder around his neck.

He walked slowly, placing each foot carefully, back to the road he'd just left. It was a mile walk, and he wasn't looking forward to it. When he left the trees, he glanced at the sky. It was still a thick, heavy gray, and he expected it to rain again soon. That would be a nuisance for which he was grateful. The worse the weather, the less likely anyone would be out. Swirling wraiths of fog drifted up from the damp asphalt, darted toward him, then disappeared in tatters, re-forming behind him as he walked. Small clouds pulsed among the trees, where the air was quieter.

The road was as straight as a geometric ideal. Anything

ahead or behind would be in a direct line with him. His ability to spot it coming was limited only by the fog. While he walked, he occasionally commented to the recorder hanging high on his chest. An observer might have thought he was mumbling to himself, like the average swamp-walking drunk.

Something swooped down on him, passed within inches of his head, and vanished in the fog. It had been a bat . . . he hoped. On either side of the road the swamp sounds seemed muted, more subdued than usual. The grunt of a bull alligator startled everything into silence for a few seconds, then the insects began again. There seemed fewer of them than he would have expected. Perhaps the rain and fog dampened their enthusiasm, or perhaps the moisture simply soaked up the sound. The tree frogs chirped away, the one thing that seemed ordinary on this most extraordinary of nights.

Three hundred yards ahead, a rutted road led back into the swamp to the left. It had taken him three weeks of cautious surveillance to learn of it. This would be his first close approach. Despite the oppressive heat, he felt a cold sweat beading on his neck and trickling down his shoulder blades. His hair was full of condensed fog, collecting in little beads around the rim of his cap and running down to his collar.

At the entrance to the side road he stopped to listen. The night sounded no different, but his next step, he knew, was irrevocable. He spoke softly into the recorder for several minutes, getting down the accumulated impressions of the last mile and freeing his mind for a new set, much like a word processor dumps an old file to disk then prepares to create a new one. The process was continuous; only the impressions changed. And David Hammond was, above all else, a word processor. In fact, he was one of the best. A Pulitzer hung on the wall of his office at the *Times Picayune*, and this story, he was convinced, could get him another one.

He entered the road with a deep sigh, trying to calm his nerves. The thumping in his chest, loud in his ears, was lost in the welter of night sounds, but he was certain it could be heard for fifty yards. A broad, shallow ditch paralleled the road on its right, and Hammond stepped into it. A startled frog bellowed before disappearing into the dank weeds behind him.

A city boy, never at ease away from the hard reassurance of concrete and plate glass, Hammond wondered why he had taken this story on. There were things in the swamp that could kill you. Alligators were only the biggest. They weren't even the most deadly. A half dozen varieties of venomous snakes, insects that carried their own poisons, quicksand—the litany went on and on. And one by one, to stifle the quivering nerves threatening to turn his feet around, whether he wanted them to or not, he ticked off the naturalist's arguments: Most snakes are more frightened of you than you are of them; insects are too small and capable of injecting too little poison to be fatal to an adult human; and quicksand was overrated, a figment of the cinematic imagination. Sure.

The road seemed endless. He checked his watch and realized he had been walking for nearly an hour. His caution had kept his progress to a minimum, but he must have gone at least a mile. He was beginning to wonder whether this hunch, titillated by scraps of rumor, was simply one more blind alley into which his reporter's curiosity had taken him on a fool's errand. It went with the territory, but the territory was seldom this malignant.

He was considering whether to call it a night when he caught a flash of illumination about two hundred yards ahead. It looked like a fog light and was surrounded by a cloudy, pale orange aura. If this wasn't what he was looking for, it was as close as he was going to be. Hammond stepped into the trees to wait. The light was stationary.

When he realized it wasn't going to get any closer, he climbed back into the ditch, now little more than a slight depression in the earth. He moved to the center of the rutted road, sidestepping some clotted grease on a patch of tall weeds at its center. He had gone about fifty yards when the light winked out. An engine roared, backfired once, then died. Hammond ducked back into the trees, creeping slowly toward the source of light and noise. A moment later he heard voices—two men, at least. One was angry, cursing at something. The other, trying to calm him, talked in a dull monotone, his voice much softer, his words less intelligible. They were coming closer.

Hammond pressed into the trees and crouched behind some dense shrubbery. He reached out to silence the last rustling leaves of his cover when two men, walking at a brisk pace, rounded a gentle curve. Both were dressed in camouflage fatigues and boots. They came and went so quickly, Hammond could see little else.

His instincts had served him well. There was a reason to look more closely. But now at least two men were between him and his car. In for a penny, in for a pound. He shrugged and started to move toward his original goal. Keeping one ear open for sounds of the men returning, he wormed his way through another hundred yards of vegetation. Keeping low and to the denser cover, he kept dislodging cascades of water. He was soaked to the skin now, but his heart was beating rapidly and his nerves were on fire. There was something here that warranted close scrutiny.

And he was the man to do it.

CHAPTER 11

Marshall Akins lay awake on his cot. The first blades of sunlight, tinted a bloody red, slashed through the slatted roof and seeped in around the small, high windows loosely covered with blackout curtains. He liked this part of the day best. He felt more alert, more alive, when he was the only one awake. He reached to the floor and snagged his watch by its band. The soft green glow of the face read 5:20.

He slipped the watch on, then lay back with his hands folded behind his head. He had the world by the tail, and he chuckled. It was a mirthless sound, more like that of a man strangling on his own tongue than one enjoying himself. In the last six months the size of the turnouts at his carefully chosen, highly orchestrated public appearances had steadily grown. The ragtag nucleus of his initial band had largely remained intact, but the hard-core center of his group had grown considerably. His mailing list was now large enough to be put on computer, and frequent mailings had begun to generate a considerable amount of cash.

But money was still the nub. Having a decent bank account to finance his activities was essential, but the more prominent he became, the more attention he drew from the jackals at the IRS. Ever since they had nailed Al Capone for income-tax evasion, Internal Revenue had been a formidable opponent. When all else failed, roust a man about his taxes. Everybody had something to hide. If you wanted to bust his chops, you could do that. If you just wanted to bust him, you could do that too. The nice thing about the IRS was how discretionary was its application . . . and its justice. Mercy was reserved for the contrite.

If there was anything Marshall Akins hated more than Communists, it was the federal government, in all its incarnations. The Postal Service couldn't deliver a goddamn letter, and although still a relatively young man, he was old enough to remember when the price of a letter was two cents. Now it was twenty-two. He also remembered when people had a say in where their kids went to school . . . and who with. If the idiots in Washington left people alone to make their own decisions, maybe a letter could be two cents again and get there in two days instead of two weeks.

He was on a roll, and he knew it. The check presentation and mortgage incineration in Downing County had been a masterstroke. For the first time, national news media were starting to notice him. Hell, if it kept up, he might even make the cover of *Time*. But the IRS was a serious problem. You couldn't very well show the man from D.C. an itemized list of weapons purchased with contributions. And you couldn't declare only part of the money, because you never knew who was watching. That left only one alternative. At first the idea of knocking over a bank had seemed too much like show business. He wanted popular sympathy, but he had no intention of becoming a latter-day Jesse James. Potential Bob Fords were a dime a dozen.

The sort of riffraff he had attracted was quite useful, within limits. But you could push that kind of luck only so far. The minute you were more valuable dead than alive to one of these Neanderthals in blue jeans was the minute you could kiss your ass good-bye. Members of the Me Generation didn't all wear pin-striped suits and sport M.B.A.'s from Wharton. "Get and spend" was a universal philosophy. Hell, wasn't it even the American Way?

So that created a need for alternative funding, as he liked to

refer to it. And that led to the recognition that a crime spree
was too risky; penny-ante stuff like that yielded too little for
too much effort. He had thought about it, even talked about it
once or twice. Some of his lieutenants were all for it. Fucking
cowboys. And that was precisely why he decided against it.

What he needed was another way to go. There had to be
one, but so far it had eluded him. He sat up, dangling his bare
feet to the floor. The light bathing the interior of the shack
splashed onto his insteps, coloring them a garish red.

Akins slipped a pair of moccasins on and stood by the bed.
He ran through a brisk series of calisthenics, then walked to
the window and drew the curtain aside. He lit a cigarette and
held the day's first inhale for a long moment. He'd been
trying to quit for several weeks, and the first drag always
made him dizzy.

Leaning toward the dusty windowpane, he brushed at an
insect, frozen against the glass. When he realized the bug was
on the other side of the window, he rapped the glass sharply
with a fingernail. The bug seemed oblivious.

Akins let the curtain fall, just as something caught his eye
at the edge of the clearing. He snatched the curtain back, but
whatever it was had disappeared. Akins grabbed a .45 automatic from its holster, hanging on the inside of the door, and
threw back the flimsy screen door to step outside.

He sprinted toward the very edge of the line of trees,
pausing in the tall weeds to listen. Heavy footsteps thudded
away, and the rustle of foliage hastily swept aside were all the
evidence he needed. Someone had been watching the camp.
He had no idea who it might have been.

For a moment he debated chasing the visitor into the
underbrush, but he had a busy schedule later that day, and he
was ill dressed for the task. He made a mental note to remind
Andy Randall to double the watch, maybe even send a patrol
out into the surrounding swamp, just in case.

Akins stood staring into the brush for several minutes. It
was just possible, he knew, that one of the more ambitious
journalists who'd been following his career had managed to
locate the camp. It bothered him to think so, since the
paramilitary right wasn't exactly popular with the left-leaning

media types. And close scrutiny of his methods was something to be avoided at all costs. The live-ammo training maneuvers would certainly attract unwelcome attention. And he sure as hell didn't want to have to explain where the guns and ammo had come from.

Thinking about it now, he was sorry he hadn't followed his instincts. That damn Tyler Hamilton had talked him into snatching the weapons, even written the phony requisition for him. Akins had wanted to go into the underground market, get whatever he needed from one of the arms traders, but Hamilton had insisted that it would be a cinch. As a colonel in the Army, Hamilton had all the clout he needed to engineer the theft, at least long enough to get the stuff under cover. Once they were underground, they might just as well have ceased to exist. Or so Hamilton had told him.

The reality had been something quite different. Two dead soldiers had been more than enough to guarantee attention. When Dan Rather had begun pontificating the night after the heist, Akins knew he'd made a serious mistake. But it was too late to turn back. Even Tyler Hamilton couldn't write a req to get him, and the stuff, back into the Ozark Armory. That milk had more than spilled; it had curdled where it lay. It was a one-way street, and there was no way to get out of it.

The sun was past the horizon now, high enough in the sky to lose its red tint. Akins watched the forest with decreasing interest, as if he'd already forgotten the intruder. He ground the cigarette under his heel, realized he should have field stripped it, then shrugged. Rules he made were rules he could ignore. Wasn't that the main reason to be at the top?

David Hammond stumbled and fell. Out of breath, he lay in the clotted weeds gasping for air. Exhausted from his all-night vigil, he was too tired even to appreciate the photographs he had just taken. When the man had first left the cabin to approach him, he had panicked. He had run several yards before he realized the explosive potential of the photo opportunity. Stopping in a clump of shrubbery, he had trained the Yashica on the man. Fiddling with the zoom lens, he had peered through the viewfinder. Not until that moment, when the blurred smear had suddenly crystallized into a sharp, clear image, had he recognized Marshall Akins. He snapped three pictures, his hands working spasmodically, working the manual film advance and struggling to control his suddenly frazzled nerves.

Now, facedown in the damp weeds, he lay on a gold mine. The pictures could go a long way to proving what he had come to believe but had so far been unable to substantiate: Marshall Akins was running a paramilitary camp in the Louisiana backcountry. The shy, gentlemanly fire-eater was a right-wing Che Guevara, training followers in the art of death, and now he could almost prove it to a certainty.

Better pictures, and some shots of the others actually running through their paces, would clinch it. He'd have to come back, but he was so excited, even that realization didn't rattle him. The story was worth every risk. He'd be back, as soon as he filed this story, this time with better equipment and a longer lens. Hammond could already visualize the next Pulitzer hanging right there alongside the first one. It might even buy him a slot on the *Washington Post* or *The New York Times*. The sky was the limit on this one, and he was the only passenger.

CHAPTER 12

Ralston's was just as loud as it had been the night before. Jake was no more at ease, but Jo had given him an opening he couldn't afford to pass up. The same two men, wearing what looked like the same khaki pants, were at the same place at the bar. This time, instead of taking a table, Jake waited for a chance to slip in beside them.

He sat on the stool, leaning heavily on his elbows, ordering a beer as soon as the bartender walked by. He listened to the men, well ahead of him in consumption, ramble away like penniless kids with their noses pressed against a candy-store window, insulting what they couldn't have.

Patiently Jake sipped his beer, then ordered another. Sooner or later they would give him a chance to put his two cents in. When it came, he wanted them to believe it was his last two cents, invested as much out of desperation as anything else.

While they talked and he waited, Jake sized them up. The taller of the two was thin and hawk-faced, with a Mediterranean nose and a dark complexion. Thick black hair, uncut for too long and combed in a style at least ten years out of date, clashed with the military cut of his clothing. Jake figured him for at least half Italian. His arms were banded with tight muscle but not the bulky kind you found on heavy lifters.

They were more like the wiry, tight muscles of a man who usually had too much work and too little to eat, a migrant worker or odd-job specialist. Jake put his age at about forty.

The second man, younger and bulkier, looked more like a fullback gone to seed. Well over two hundred pounds, he looked stronger but softer. In a pinch Jake would have wanted hawk-face on his side a lot sooner. He was somewhere in his late twenties, that pale, thin hair of Celtic stock cut short and already showing too much scalp for somebody so young. His skin was a bright red, as if he weren't used to the harsh southern sun.

The younger man was immediately on Jake's right. His speech, delivered in a reedy, whining voice, was already slurred, and his movements were slightly out of kilter. Reaching for a cigarette, he knocked Jake's beer over, soaking the bar and the pack of Luckys. He turned to survey the damage, weaving the least little bit. He apologized and hollered for the bartender to give Jake another beer.

"Don't worry about it," Jake said. "No problem."

"No, no, no. I knocked the fucking thing over. I can buy you another one. I got plenty of money, man." The older man jabbed him with an elbow, and he nearly fell over.

Hawk-face leaned in and said, "We just got paid. Junior, here, likes to drink it all up in one night. Don't pay no attention to him."

"That's okay. I know how it is. I've done more than my share of hard work. And got little enough to show for it too."

Hawk-face stuck his hand across the midriff of his younger companion. "Name's Marcelli, Peter Marcelli. This lump of meat is Brian Riley, Jr. We call him Junior, kind of like a pet name, you know. He's nothing but a big puppy dog, anyways. And about as smart. Almost."

Jake took the hand and shook it. The grip confirmed his initial impression. The guy was as hard as nails. "Name's Jake O'Bannion. Look, let me buy you guys a drink. I don't know anybody here, just passing through. It's nice to shake a friendly hand."

"Know what you mean. This is hard country. Man don't have money, he don't have friends, either. It's the same back

East. I guess it's a little easier to take out here, but not much.''

"Where you from, originally?"

"Rego Park. Queens."

"You're shitting me. I'm from Brooklyn, Sheepshead Bay."

"Hear that, Junior?" Marcelli said, nudging Riley again. "The man's from my hometown. The Big Apple."

"The Apple's got a couple of worms in it, you ask me," Jake mumbled.

"Two less since me and you split, huh?" Marcelli laughed bitterly.

"What the hell are you doing in Arkansas?"

"Oh, nothing much. Just passing through, actually. Got a job in Louisiana. How about you?"

"Same with me. Only I don't have a job."

"What sort of work do you do?" Marcelli asked.

"Anything that pays," Jake answered. "Long as it pays, I can handle it. Been that way since the Marines, really. Seems like people don't give a shit about vets anymore. Used to be, you were respected, had a leg up, you know? The country paid you back for what you did. Not anymore."

"Marines, huh? When was that?"

"Early sixties."

"You were lucky, Jake. You missed all the fun in Vietnam. That's where I did my time. Army, but hell, there wasn't much difference. We were all meat for the lions."

"I know. Two of my best buddies bought it over there. They were lifers. Best friends a man could want." Jake shook his head. He was telling the truth, simply modifying it slightly to fit the current need.

"You look like you're in pretty good shape, though." Marcelli hauled Riley to one side to change places with the younger man. "You got a bit of a gut there." He rapped Jake in the belly with his knuckles. "But, hell, you could work that off in a week, you wanted to."

"You got a job for me?"

"Just might could be. We ought to talk some." Marcelli looked over Jake's shoulder toward the tables. Spotting an empty one, he tugged Jake's sleeve. "Come on, let's grab a seat. Junior, bring the beers."

Two hours later Marcelli got up, making a show of his beneficence. "Let me make a couple of calls. I think we just might be able to work something out for you and your friend. I mean, if white men don't stick together, we'll really be in deep shit, right?"

"I'd really appreciate it, Pete."

"No sweat. I'll be back in a few minutes. Want to run over to the hotel to make the calls." He winked. "More private, know what I mean?"

"I'll keep an eye on Junior."

"If he falls over, just keep him out of people's way."

When Marcelli was gone, Jake called Jo over to order a cup of coffee and a hamburger.

"You make friends fast, don't you?" She seemed put out.

"Not as fast as I'd like."

"That's your fault. Where were you this afternoon? I thought we were going to have lunch."

"Oh, Jesus, was that today? I got confused."

"Or maybe I don't look so good in the cold light of day. Is that it?"

"No way. I just got wrapped up in things, and it slipped my mind."

"Yeah? What sort of things you wrapped up in? With Sheriff Hodges?"

Jake put a finger to his lips, nodding toward the sleeping Junior. "I'll tell you later. What time do you get off?"

"I haven't gotten off in so long, I'm not sure I'd remember." She smiled seductively.

"We'll have to see what we can do about that." Jake rolled his eyes, a parody of the silent-screen lecher.

"You're pretty sure of yourself, aren't you?"

"And you're not?"

Jo looked pensively at the table. "No, I'm not," she said after a long pause. "And I'm not sure about you, either. But beggars can't be choosers."

"Jo, darlin', the day you have to beg will be a black day indeed for the race."

"I'll see you at one o'clock. You still have the address?"

"Tattooed on my hard heart."

"So, the Blarney Stone still works, does it, Mr. O'Bannion?"

"Why, whatever do you mean?"

She laughed and turned away. Jake watched her go, the delicate swivel of her hips well oiled and a joy to behold. For a minute he felt bad about deceiving her, then wondered whether he was. She was a big girl. And he *was* fond of her, fonder than he cared to admit.

Before he could dwell on it, Junior rolled his head to one side, knocking a glass to the floor. The crash woke him up, and he tried to sit up. The struggle exhausted whatever reserves of energy he had, and a moment later his head crashed back to the table. Jake smiled to himself. He'd been there more than once himself. And he didn't envy Junior his morning head.

Marcelli was back, grinning from ear to ear. "It's all set. When can your friend get here?"

"Hell, for a shot like this, he'll be here tomorrow. I guarantee it."

"I'm counting on it. We got to roll out by tomorrow night. We're due back day after."

"We'll meet you here tomorrow night then, all right?"

"Check."

"You need any help with Junior, there?"

"Hell, I been lugging the damn fool half across the country and back for so long, I can do it in my sleep. Can I borrow this?" He hefted Jake's beer in his right hand.

"Suit yourself."

"Thanks. This usually works." He tilted Junior's head to one side and poured some cold beer in the unconscious man's ear. Junior groaned, swept one hand up as if to chase away a bug, then sat straight up. The remains of the beer dribbled down his collar, and he shuddered.

"Damn, did I pass out again, Pete?"

"When don't you?"

Junior grinned lopsidedly at both men. "You right. Sorry."

"All right, Jake. See you tomorrow." He hauled Junior to

his feet, and staggering slightly with his unsteady partner held under one arm, he headed for the door.

Jo, the hamburger and coffee balanced on one hand, braced her free hand on one hip. She stood looking after the staggering men for a minute, then turned to Jake. "Nice friends you managed to make."

"Thanks. I try." A beatific smile flashed across Jake's features. "The new boy in town can't be choosy. Just drop that burger and I'll see you later, all right?"

"You'd better." She gave Jake her sternest scowl before walking off.

The elevator groaned as it wobbled up the shaft to the third floor. Jake walked softly down the hall, reaching for his hotel key. At the door he paused for a moment, his ear to the panel. It was an old habit, but it had served him well for too long to let go. Satisfied, he inserted the key, opened the door, and stepped inside.

Before the light went on, he had a funny feeling, the sensation of being watched. He turned to look down the hall, but no one was in sight. He looked at the door directly across from his own, but it was tightly closed, and there was no peephole. He clicked the light on and stepped in.

He knew immediately why he had felt odd. The room was a shambles. His suitcase, upended, lay in the middle of the floor. His clothes were a rumpled litter around the room, draped over furniture and lying in balls on the floor. Jake reached for his gun and, cocking it, walked toward the closet. He yanked it open, but it was empty. He stepped to the closed bathroom door and felt it with his fingertips. It was unlatched. He pushed softly, and the door swung back.

The bathroom, too, had been tossed. His shaving gear lay in the sink; the towels and facecloths lay in a pile in the tub. Whoever did it had been more than thorough and used to searching in a hurry.

He was out most of the day, so there had been ample opportunity for the intruders to do their work, but they hadn't known that. He immediately thought of Marcelli. He'd been gone a half hour, more than enough time. And who else would

have felt confident of Jake's whereabouts, confident enough
to slip in and take a look around? Who else even would have
had reason?

Jake picked a few things off the floor, then decided to call
Luke earlier than planned. He'd picked up the phone and
started to dial when a thought struck him. He replaced the
phone in its cradle and turned the instrument over. A few
fresh scratches on the cover plate told him all he needed to
know. Grabbing some change from the floor, where it had
fallen, Jake left the room and went back to the lobby. Out in
the street, he headed away from the hotel. He needed a pay
phone.

It was just one more wrinkle in an already untidy mess.

CHAPTER 13

"All right, let's put all the pieces on the table." Luke was in his no-bullshit mode. Dressed down for the occasion, he paced restlessly, hands clenched behind his back. Old jeans and a threadbare work shirt could not quite conceal the essence of the man, but he was trying.

"Well," Jake began, "let me tell you what I've got. First, as near as I can tell, this guy Marcelli had something to do with the bank job here. He belongs to some group or other, but he was real cautious. I don't know the name, and I don't know who runs it."

"Tran's analysis established that the weapons used in the bank job were definitely taken from the Ozark Armory. That means that whoever killed those two men and took down the bank also killed two men at the armory and has some connections we don't know about."

"I can guess the connection," Jake said. "Jo Mason, that's the waitress I told you about, says there's a bunch of these far-right kind of groups pretty active in the area. They all have pretty much the same philosophy, but some of them are just big talkers and some of them are a lot worse than that."

"We can do a lot worse than hang with this guy Marcelli,"

Luke suggested. "Even if his group isn't the one we want, it very probably is tied in. Most of them have overlapping membership, and they all talk to one another. It's like the old Hollywood movies where the mobsters sit down to carve up Chicago. If we can get close to one of them, get inside, then we have a good shot at going all the way. Sooner or later somebody is going to say something we can use."

"It's gonna be a tense few days, Luke. We're gonna hear a lot of shit we're not gonna like. We might even have to say some of it ourselves. It'll look funny unless we try to come on even stronger than they do. We've got to seem real anxious to belong, you know."

"Come on, Jake, you've been undercover before. Acting is part of the program, you know that."

"Maybe so, but this is different. This is real mean shit. I have a feeling I'm not gonna meet anybody I like for quite a while."

"Hell, you don't like too many people, anyway."

"You should talk. Mr. High-tech Hermit. You had your way, you wouldn't talk to anyone or anything that didn't have at least a few microchips for a brain."

"Saves back talk, Jake. Garbage in, garbage out, remember?"

"Okay, okay."

"Tell me about Marcelli."

"Not much to tell, really. Near as I can figure, he's bummed around since the service. He was in 'Nam, got a taste for military stuff, and doesn't seem capable of making a decision. He'd rather have somebody do it for him."

"I need more than that."

"That's about all there is. You know the type. Guy doesn't have much on the ball, no skills, drinks a little too much a little too often. Mean temper. Probably got his ass fired from every job he's ever had. He's a textbook case of what the Marines call 'bad attitude.' "

"What about the other guy, Junior?"

"Mr. Shit-for-brains. The guy doesn't know which end is up. Perfect cannon fodder. The kind of kid you send in to foul the other team's big scorer. He takes him out, fine; you lose him, that's okay too."

"You sure about that?"

"As near as I can tell, he's a decent enough kid, but he'll listen to whoever talked to him last. Mental quadriplegic, really. A fucking zombie. Only he's got muscles up the wazoo. Know what I mean?"

"Sounds like a hell of a team."

"What do you want from me?"

"What time do we meet Marcelli?"

Jake checked his watch. "About an hour. He'll pick us up at Ralston's."

"Why don't we grab something to eat? I'd like to get a look at this new friend of yours."

"Hands off."

"It sounds serious."

"When you're my age, serious is something you read about. I like her. A lot. She's had a tough time lately, but she's got a lot of spunk. I guess I kind of admire her."

"That's good enough for me. I think the last woman you admired was Cleopatra."

"It hasn't been that long, has it? Jesus!"

"Pretty near."

"And you had to remind me, right? Damn, Luke, you know what your problem is? You like to bust chops. You can't resist."

"It's part of my charm."

"Your ass, boss. It's the sum total of your charm."

Luke slapped Jake on the back. "You all packed?"

"Yeah. I didn't bring much, anyhow, and where we're going I won't even need that, from what Marcelli tells me. What about you?"

"I'm set. I got a few goodies in my bag. Fake bottom, just in case."

Junior Riley was still in bed. His head ached, his tongue felt like a razor strop. A rush of shower water from the bathroom roared in his ears like a captive Niagara, abrading every nerve. The harsh overhead light seared his retinas, even through closed lids, filling his head with fire. He shook his head slowly from side to side. The blur across the room slowly crystallized into a mirror, reflecting the bare bulb. He squeezed his lids even tighter, smearing everything with a pale red shot through with brilliant flashes.

He knew it was time to get up, and he didn't want to. He also knew that Marcelli would lean on him hard if he didn't. He sat up and opened his eyes. As his feet touched the floor, everything started to swim, the room was spinning. He felt like he'd fallen into a whirlpool. He closed his eyes again and took a deep breath. His churning stomach began to settle, and he opened his eyes again. This time everything was wavy but stayed in place.

Junior stood up, supporting himself on the creaking metal bedstead, its chipped paint rough under his fingers. The whole room reeked of a sour smell, and he wasn't sure whether it was simply an olfactory sensation or emanated from something unspeakable someplace in the room. He didn't really want to know.

While he struggled to keep his balance, the shower stopped. Marcelli stepped out of the bathroom, a towel secured around his waist sari-style.

"Junior, you look like something the cat wouldn't even bother to drag in."

"I love you, too, Pete. What time is it?"

"About three o'clock, I guess. You better haul ass. We have to pick up the new guys in a couple of hours. Time to get rolling."

"What about the money?"

"What about it?"

"We gonna leave it here?"

"Don't worry about it. It's safe. I sure as hell ain't gonna give it to Akins. He's got plenty."

"He finds out about it, he'll have your ass, and mine too."

"Look, don't worry about it. He won't find out. Not unless you tell him. Because I sure as hell won't."

"What are we going to tell him about Perkins?"

"We been through that. We tell him Perkins run off with some woman. He'll believe that. And he won't bother to look for him. Hell, he didn't even like Perkins. He'll be just as happy the asshole's gone."

"I still think we should have give him a chance."

"What could we do? The idiot got himself shot. We couldn't very well take him to a hospital. We couldn't lug him around with us, neither. It was the only way. Besides, if we brought him home, Akins would figure it out. Trust me, Junior, we done what we had to."

"I sure hope you're right."

"When am I not?"

"Where'd you hide the money?"

"It's safe."

"Where?"

"Don't worry about it."

"We'll come back for it in a couple of months. I didn't even count it."

"Paper says it was over seven hundred thousand dollars."

"Paper says, paper says . . . Junior, I already told you, don't believe nothing you read in the damn paper. Them bankers are always saying shit to the papers. Usually they just tack on what they took for themselves. Hell, I'd be surprised if we got two hundred grand."

"Looked like more than that to me, Pete."

"You don't know nothing, Junior. Get dressed."

"You sure it's a good idea to bring Jake with us?"

" 'Course I'm sure. I wouldn't do it otherwise."

"You ask Mr. Akins about it?"

"I don't have to ask him about it. Besides, I talked to Andy Randall."

"I don't know . . . ."

"Junior, you're right. You *don't* know. Trouble with you is you think small. For a big kid, you got the smallest brain I know of. I swear to God. You want to make something of yourself, you got to go ahead and do it. Don't wait for nobody to tell you it's okay. 'Cause he never will. Never."

"And what if we haul Jake and his friend all the way down there and Mr. Akins don't like it. What then?"

"What the hell do you mean, 'What then?' "

"What happens to Jake?"

"Who cares? He don't have a job now, anyhow. What the hell's the difference whether he's out of luck in Arkansas or

Louisiana? That's like trying to tell the difference between pig shit and cow shit. It still stinks. I mean, Jake's all right, and I don't want to bust his hump for nothing. But he's a bug boy. He can take care of hisself.''

"I hope you know what you're doing, that's all."

"Don't worry about it. It's no skin off your ass, anyhow. If Akins doesn't like it, I'll handle it, that's all. Now get dressed, will you, for chrissake? If you don't get a move on, ain't *nobody* going to Louisiana."

Junior grumbled under his breath. Marcelli, tired of the conversation and firmly convinced that Junior was beyond education of any sort, didn't bother to react. It wouldn't do any good, and they were already behind schedule.

CHAPTER 14

Tyler Hamilton stared out of the window of his car, watching the lights fracture into small comets in the water running off the roof. He glanced at the dim glow of the digital clock mounted in the dash and cursed softly. He'd already been waiting for more than a half hour, and he had things to do.

It was too late to second-guess himself, he knew that. But that didn't mean he shouldn't have misgivings. He should have known better than to get mixed up with amateurs, no matter how well-meaning. Some things were better left to professionals, and then only if you couldn't do them yourself.

A pair of dull spots appeared in the rearview mirror. He sat up and watched the car approach. It was moving slowly, as if the driver weren't certain of what he was looking for.

"Come on, come on, move your ass," Hamilton mumbled. The car ignored him, continuing its slow, steady drift toward him. To control his impatience he began counting by twos. By the time he got to a hundred, the car had come to a halt about twenty feet behind him. He blinked his lights twice in quick succession. The new arrival responded with three flashes of its own.

A moment later the passenger door opened. In the brief glimmer from the dome light, Hamilton noticed the distinctive

baby-blue color of the big Lincoln. He'd repeatedly warned
Akins not to use the car for sensitive meetings, because it was
too easy to spot, but the bastard had a stubborn streak as wide
as the monstrous car's grille. And there were bigger problems
to worry about, now that things had gotten so out of control.

Akins leaned down to look through the passenger window,
and Hamilton leaned over to unlock the door. Akins, smelling
of rainwater and expensive cologne, slipped in and slammed
the door shut behind himself.

"Where the hell were you?" Hamilton exploded. "I've
been waiting almost an hour."

"I had some last-minute business to attend to. I'm a busy
man, in case you haven't read the papers lately."

"Oh, yes, I've read the papers. Maybe you shouldn't read
them so often. It seems to me you're too busy building your
image to pay attention to critical details."

"Like what?"

"Don't act dumb with me, Akins. It's too close to
typecasting."

"I don't know what you're so upset about," Akins said.
He tried to sound hurt, but there was too much self-satisfaction
in his voice for him to pull it off.

"We don't have enough time for me to tell you everything
I'm upset about, so I'll just deal with the major points."

"Shoot," Akins said, leaning back in the seat like a bored
miscreant making his umpteenth visit to the principal's office.

"I should shoot . . . you."

"Why?" Akins seemed genuinely surprised.

"Everything was arranged for you. It couldn't have been
simpler. And you fucked up."

"You mean the armory?"

"What else? How in the hell could you let that happen?
Do you have any idea of the trouble you've caused? There are
no fewer than six separate agencies looking into that little
fiasco."

"So? I thought you were Mr. Fix It. I thought you were
plugged into the highest circles. That should be a piece of
cake."

"Not with two men dead, it isn't. I can fix it, but it won't be easy. And some people don't even want it fixed. They want *you* fixed."

Akins lit a cigarette and puffed nervously. "Roll the window down a little, will you? It's too damn stuffy in here."

When Hamilton buzzed the window down, Akins flipped the butt in a low arc off into the weeds alongside the car. He heard it hiss as it winked out in the rain. "What else?" he asked.

"Your profile is too high."

"My what?"

"Your profile. You're attracting too much attention, not much of it good. That's got to stop."

"What kind of attention? A little national coverage can't hurt, surely. It confers a little legitimacy. *Heartlanders* is getting to be a household word."

"And on the heels of celebrity, my naïve friend, comes scrutiny. We can't afford that. Not now."

"Not until you fix it, you mean."

"Partly."

"Then fix it." Akins, fortified by his recollection of the press coverage, was recovering his spunk.

"I will. But I want *you* to do your part too. I want you to cut down on your personal appearances for a while."

"For how long?" Alarmed, Akins sat up straight, bumping his head on the low roof of the car.

"I'll let you know."

Akins stared glumly at the rain, not speaking. When it was obvious he had nothing to say, Hamilton continued. "Your choice of lieutenants leaves more than a little to be desired as well. Something will have to be done about that."

Akins snapped his head to the left to stare directly at Hamilton. "What are you talking about? Who?"

"A little matter of a bank robbery in Arkansas—Ferris, Arkansas, to be exact. I trust you know the town?"

"You know damn well I do. It's only fifteen miles from the farm. But I don't know anything about any bank robbery."

"I'm sure you don't. But you should. That you don't is just one more thing making my associates nervous."

"Fuck your associates. Fuck you too. Why the hell should I give a damn about some jerkwater bank, no matter where it is?"

Hamilton didn't answer immediately. Akins had the distinct impression he was letting him stew a little before continuing. When he spoke again, Hamilton changed the subject.

"Were the guns delivered to the farm, as they were supposed to be?"

"Yes."

"All of them?"

"All of them, yes."

"You're absolutely certain about that?"

"Yes, dammit, I'm absolutely certain about that. What the hell is your problem, Hamilton?"

"Who made the delivery?"

"Peter Marcelli."

"Who else?"

"Why are you asking me all these dumb questions?"

"Indulge me a little, won't you, Marshall? You have known me long enough to know I have my reasons."

"I'm beginning to wonder."

Hamilton abruptly dropped the genteel veneer. "Who else, dammit? I asked you a question. Answer it. Now!"

"Junior Riley and Ralph Perkins."

"And where are they now?"

"At the camp."

"All three?"

"Well, not exactly."

Hamilton sighed deeply. He rolled his window down and stuck his arm out into the rain. In silence he watched rainwater accumulate in his palm. The surface of the clear fluid, repeatedly fractured by falling rain and brilliantly lit by the floodlight across the road, splattered bright jewels through his fingers, where they vanished into the darkness.

"Be precise, please, Marshall," he continued. "It's very important that I know."

"Perkins didn't come back."

"Where is he?"

"He went home. He got fed up, he was tired of the camp."

"He told you this himself?"

"No. He told Marcelli, and Marcelli told me."

"It may interest you to know he did *not* go home. It may also interest you to know that he is no longer among the living. Does it interest you, Marshall?"

"Hamilton, I'm tired, and I really don't need your dime-store theatrics. Why the fuck can't you quit playing games and come right out and say what you mean for once?"

"Very well, then, I shall. Ralph Perkins is dead. His body has been found in the woods outside of Ferris. Near the farm, I might add."

"Dead, how?"

"Shot to death. The interesting, and I think pertinent, facts are these: He was shot with two different weapons, a .45-caliber automatic, not coincidentally the type of weapon used by one William McCallum, a guard at the Ferris bank. Mr. McCallum is also dead, by the way, as is the president of the bank, whose name doesn't matter. The other gun was an M16. As it happens, the very type being taken to the farm. The recovered bullets, curiously enough, came from the ammunition recently stolen from the Ozark Armory. I needn't tell you any more about that. The third matter of interest is that the money has not been recovered and the robbers have not been caught."

"And you think Perkins was involved in the bank robbery?"

"It has been scientifically established to a certainty. Beyond that, all is conjectural, but since that is my stock-in-trade, let me tell you what I think happened."

Hamilton paused to light a cigarette. He let the smoke drift in a small cloud in front of him, watching it with detachment for several seconds before continuing. "Perkins, Marcelli, and Riley, without authorization, committed the robbery. In the process Perkins was wounded by the guard. It was not prudent to have his wound treated or to travel with him. So Marcelli and Riley solved their problem in the most expedient fashion. They eliminated Mr. Perkins, not coincidentally increasing their personal shares from the robbery by a considerable amount.''

"Are you sure about this?"

"As sure as I feel I ought to be."

"Now what?"

Hamilton sighed. "Marshall, sometimes I wonder about you. I should think the answer to that question is obvious."

"Oh? And what is it, if it's so obvious?"

"Mr. Marcelli and Mr. Riley have to be taught a lesson. And we expect you to teach them."

"Don't worry about it. I'll handle it."

"Soon would be best, I should think."

"I said I'll handle it."

CHAPTER 15

David Hammond was struggling. Still not used to the word-processing consoles the paper had installed, ostensibly to make everyone's work easier, he kept losing text. Years of banging away at an old Royal, hard as nails and capable as a bulldozer of pushing back, had left him feeling more than a little anachronistic. The younger journalists, raised on apples, and schooled on Apples, were far more at ease.

He marked a text block, pushed the requisite sequence of keys, and held his breath. When the screen flickered, then rolled, he cursed out loud, then, when the story was rearranged, just as he had wanted it, he heaved a long sigh. He was home free. All he needed now was a tight, neat little paragraph to wrap the whole bundle, and he could go home for a few hours sleep.

His neck, a welter of insect bites, itched like hell. He had doused it repeatedly in calamine lotion and cortisone cream, but nothing seemed to work. The window was open wide, since the paper had seen fit to install automation rather than much-needed air-conditioning. The harder he struggled with the story, the more he sweated. The more he sweated, the more irritated his neck became. Rubbing it in anger and from nervous habit had only aggravated matters.

For four days, ever since his first story on Heartlanders had been picked up by the wire services, he'd been frightened. He was certain he had been followed, but whenever he did a quick turn or popped into an alley to get the drop on his pursuers, he'd seen nothing. But paranoia was nothing new for him. It went with the territory.

He remembered what happened to the poet, Ed Sanders, after he started his book on the Manson family. There was no way of telling who was watching you and who was just innocently passing by. The more nervous you got, the more suspects you found.

Hammond wanted to shrug his shoulders and forget it, but he knew how fatalistic it was to look into this kind of story. If you spent all your time looking over your shoulder, you never saw what was right in front of your nose.

Hammond wanted to be like Seymour Hersh, or Woodward and Bernstein, digging in with tooth and nail and letting the horse run with the wind. But he needed a new angle, some hook into Akins to rip his flesh a little. If he could bloody him, he could get a little help. Put him on edge and he would falter. One step would be enough. But every lead followed, every seemingly loose strand tugged free, had been effort wasted.

Even the photographs he'd managed were useless. Underexposed because of the poor light, they showed a blur that was only conjecturally a man. He was going back, but not for a couple of days. And his editor was getting impatient.

The clicking keys finally began to fall into a rhythm he could understand. The hypnotic flicker of the cursor no longer distracted his eye. The words started to come, and they fell easily into place. The story was almost writing itself. As the final paragraph grew to three, and then to five, times its intended length, Hammond knew he had found the heart of the story at last. His fingers flew over the keyboard until even the click of the keys was an undifferentiated jumble of sounds, white noise, part of the environment.

When he finally ran out of steam, Hammond sat back, read it over twice, corrected a few typos, and filed it. He sighed, then finished his coffee, crunching the cup into a ball and tossing it into the nearest wastebasket. He slipped a disk into the workstation, duped his story, slipped the disk into his jacket pocket, and got up. It was too hot to wear the jacket, so he slung it over his shoulder and turned off the power at his console.

Nate, the night man, was on the elevator. "You working kind of late these days, ain't you, Mr. Hammond?"

"Yeah, I guess so, Nate. The new equipment, you know. It takes some getting used to."

"Know what you mean, Mr. Hammond. Same thing happened to me. I remember when we took the stairs out and put in this here elevator. Took me a couple of months to figure it out."

"Cut it out, Nate. It's too late for that kind of stuff."

"Never too late for a grin, Mr. Hammond. Never too late for a grin."

"I guess you're right, Nate. See you tomorrow."

The elevator clanked to a halt, and Hammond stepped out into the deserted lobby. The door ground closed behind him, then the elevator whined back up the shaft, creaking on its cables. Hammond shook his head. The elevator was probably older than Nate.

His feet rapped sharply on the polished marble floor. He stopped at the newsstand, its wire grate down and locked. He wanted to buy cigarettes, but it would have to wait. He nodded good night to the guard, doing a crossword puzzle at his station, just inside the revolving door. He stepped in, pushed the glass, and a blast of hot air slammed him in the face as he reached the street.

Across the way, high on the Reynolds Building, a digital clock/thermometer alternated between 2:29 A.M. and 84°F. At least it wasn't Celsius. That would be too much progress for him to handle in one day. Eighty-four degrees was hot by any standard. And he didn't care what anybody said, it sure as hell was the heat, regardless of the humidity.

His car was parked four blocks away in the all-night municipal garage. He hesitated for a minute, trying to remember which way would take him past the all-night newsstand. Turning to the left, he reached Huey Long Boulevard, turned right, and walked two blocks to the newsstand. The blind man who ran it seemed always to be there, day and night.

He asked for a pack of Marlboros, changed it to Marlboro Lights, and watched the educated fingers of the proprietor dance on the green steel racks, find the right pack, and yank it out with a hiss of cellophane.

"One twenty-five."

"How come you're so much cheaper than the other places?" Hammond asked.

"That way folks feel like they getting a bargain. Don't have to cheat the old blind man."

"That's a novel approach to commerce," David said.

"Commerce, hell! It's just good business. You run a place like this a few years, you don't need no M.B.A."

"I suppose not," Hammond said.

"Suppose, my ass. That's the truth, man."

David handed the old man two wrinkled bills, then watched the fingers, equally wrinkled, deftly extract the correct change from his coin tray. "Thanks. Good night!"

" 'Night your own self. It's always night for me. And Ray Charles." The sharp laughter didn't sound as bitter as it might have.

Hammond slipped the cellophane from the box, noted the accordioned corner of the pack, wondered how they could get away with calling it "crush-proof," then realized it just didn't make any difference. Not to anyone.

He waited for the light at the next corner. Lighting a cigarette, he waited for a newspaper delivery truck to run the amber signal, then stepped out into the intersection. On the far curb, he thought he heard something just ahead. He moved to the outside edge of the curb.

Striding quickly, he passed a deep entryway, glancing in. His nerves quieted when he noticed a wino coiled in a tight ball, rustling in some crumpled sheets of wrapping paper. He quickened his pace, covering the rest of the block at a near run. He dashed across the intersection as the light changed.

Moving down the last block, he heard muffled footsteps and ducked into a narrow hallway. A moment later two black teenagers sprinted past. Their jogging suits were damp. They had been running for quite a while.

Hammond laughed at his anxiety, suppressing the shuddering chill between his shoulder blades. He stepped back onto the sidewalk, moving briskly toward the corner. Turning right, he saw the garage marquee, its garish yellow and green neon splattering the street and the buildings opposite with a nervous dance of color.

He entered the ramp, stopping for a moment to check the street behind him. It was still deserted. Nodding to the gate attendant in his cupola, Hammond turned to the ramp, choosing to walk straight up the middle of the helical garage level by level, rather than trust his luck to the narrow stairwells. The caged bulbs were usually half broken at the best of times, and shadow was the last thing he wanted to walk through.

On level two he reached into his pocket for the car key. It tinkled on its chain, a laquered Kachina rapping against the keys as it balanced their weight on the other side of his index finger. Another half coil and he spotted the familiar dent in the left rear fender of his red Audi. He'd been meaning to get it fixed for more than a month, but time was at a premium. The car was his connection. He couldn't afford to have it out of service for three or four days, and Walters had really busted his hump over the one-night rental of the black Toyota.

Hammond stopped, slapping his pocket once to make sure he still had the pack of Marlboro Lights. He did a quick three-sixty and, seeing no one, sprinted the last twenty yards to the Audi.

He kept his eyes on the row of cars ahead as he slipped the key in, yanked open the door, and half fell into the bucket seat. He slammed the door sharply, banged the electric lock, and sat back with a sigh.

Home free one more night. If something didn't break on the story soon, his nerves were going to short out.

He inserted the ignition key, turned it, and cursed at the click followed by stony silence. It sounded like his battery was gone. He tried again. Again the starter relay clicked, but this time the Audi roared. It rose in sections, a dismembered flower blooming in stop action and decaying in a colorful splash. The bomb took off all four doors and ignited the fuel almost instantaneously.

In David Hammond's pocket, the computer disk puckered, crackled, and finally burst into flame. It would not even be noticed among the ashes.

CHAPTER 16

"So, where you from, Lou?" Marcelli glanced at Luke over the back of the front seat.

"New Mexico."

"Oh, yeah. I never been there. What's it like?"

"Depends. You got money, it's like anyplace else. You don't, it's like anyplace else."

"I know what you mean. Money makes the world go round, right?"

"Far as I can see."

Luke affected a laconic style, keeping conversation to a minimum. Using the name Lou Simmons, Jake had introduced him to Marcelli and Junior. Marcelli, obviously nervous about something, had been chattering for two hours, and Luke was letting him run, sifting through the mindless wordstream for nuggets of meaningful information.

So far the only thing he had been able to conclude was that Marcelli, not unexpectedly, liked to exaggerate his own role in every activity he'd been involved in. Taken with a good-sized grain of salt, there was little left over of much value.

"You're going to like Marshall Akins, Lou. Greatest man I ever met. Best day of my life, the day I hooked up with him.

I think I've been pretty good for him, too, but he'll probably tell you all about that.''

"How'd you meet him?" Luke asked.

"Friend of mine, guy named Ralph Perkins, introduced us. Ralph'd been with him right from the beginning. We hit it off, and I been with him for three years now.''

Junior turned to look at Luke and opened his mouth to speak when Marcelli rapped him on the shoulder. "Watch the goddamn road, Junior. All we need is for you to run us into a tree.''

"You want to drive?" Junior asked.

"I'm busy talking to Lou and Jake. You tend to your business, make sure we get home in one piece. That's enough for you to handle, God knows." Marcelli laughed, turning back to Luke. "Junior can do two things at once, long as they're both simple. Breathing is one, so that don't leave him many options.''

Luke smiled. He tilted a John Deere cap low over his eyes and hunched down in the seat. From under the bill of the cap he said, "I'm gonna catch a few winks. I'm bushed. Wake me when we get there.''

"Your buddy's kind of low on stamina, ain't he, Jake?" Marcelli laughed.

"We had a long night, if you know what I mean," Jake answered.

"Must've been drinkin', then. There weren't no women worth a second look in that burg.''

"How long were you guys there?"

"Few days," Marcelli answered. "Two, three maybe.''

Jake recognized the evasion for what it was. Four days would have put them in town long enough to be involved in the robbery of the Ferris bank. "I guess I'll get a little sleep, too, Pete," Jake said.

"You can't handle the sauce, you ought to stay away from it, Jake. Take Junior, here. He can't handle it, either. I keep telling him, drink soda and find a teenybopper, but he don't listen. He wants to drink with the men and run after the women. He ever gets lucky, I think it'll kill him.''

"Fuck you," Junior growled.

"You may have to, the way things are goin' for you lately." Mercifully Marcelli shut up, then leaned against the window ledge on the passenger side.

Jake watched him through slitted eyes.

It was near dawn when Luke awoke. Dark gray masses of trees were zipping by on either side of the road. Marcelli was driving now, and the dim bulk huddled against the passenger door would be Junior. Luke kept silent, watching the edge of the road for signs, anything that might give him a hint where they were. All Marcelli would tell him was that they were going to a camp in Louisiana.

Luke flashed back to his Company days and remembered the training camps established by the CIA for anti-Castro Cubans. They were in the backcountry, along Lake Pontchartrain. It was a great choice, because you'd have to look a long time to find anyplace in the continental U.S. in which it was easier to hide. There was little tourism, and the locals, what few there were, had a long tradition of minding their own business.

For a moment Luke wondered whether Akins and the Company were connected. He'd have to pull a few strings to find out, but it just might be worth the trouble. The dark gray was beginning to brighten, and the engine of the car, a big Oldsmobile, thrummed steadily. Luke could feel the vibration through the floorboards and guessed they were doing near eighty.

So far there had been neither a break in the line of trees nor a sign. Somewhere behind them, he knew, was Ben Sanchez. Following the signal from a transmitter in Luke's bag was the only alternative. Ben was good, but it would be a bitch of a job under the best of circumstances.

Ben was already following some tenuous strands connecting Akins to a clique of super-patriotic Army officers, mostly captains and above, but so far not reaching as high as general. Probably career frustrations had turned their energies elsewhere. Nobody ever wanted to see himself as the problem, so he looked outside for enemies, some nebulous, shadowy "they" who were ruining things. Add that to the action orientation of the military mind and you had the makings for some serious trouble.

Luke had seen it more than once in Central and South America, even during his relatively short stint at CIA. Most military coups involved greedy have-not junior officers who disguised their lust for the fruits of the good life under a militant patriotism and rabid anti-Communist stance. The U.S. was not immune to that sort of thing but so far had been lucky. Luke shuddered to think what might happen the day that luck ran out.

The car lurched suddenly, throwing the still sleeping Jake into him. O'Bannion groaned and sat up, rubbing his eyes. Luke, too, admitted to being awake.

"I wonder how Junior would have taken that turn?" Jake murmured.

"You shitting me, Jake?" Marcelli laughed. "With Junior behind the wheel, we'd *all* be sleeping now, permanently, 'stead of just him."

"What time is it?"

"Almost six. We'll be there in a few minutes."

Jake looked out the window at the forest, now beginning to come to life. "Where the hell are we?"

"Lou-ee-zee-anna! Home of jambalaya and Ron Guidry. That's all you need to know."

"I hope to Christ I don't have to *walk* out of here," Jake said.

"Don't even think about that, Jake. You here, you here to stay, baby. This place is so goddamn special, you won't want to leave, and if you do, we can't let you, anyhow. Besides, Marshall'd have my ass if I brought you here and let you walk away. We can't have that, now can we?"

"I didn't say I wanted to, Pete. I just said I hoped I didn't have to. How the hell do you eat? Where do you get a drink? This is a fucking no-man's-land."

" 'Course it is. Why do you think we picked it?"

"How'd you know about it?" Luke asked.

"Friend of Akins told him about it. Used to be a CIA training camp. You know, maneuvers, Bay of Pigs invasion, that kind of shit."

"Akins is CIA?"

"Hell, I don't know what he is. Them CIA guys never tell you anything straight, anyhow. But what difference does it make? You get three squares a day and a place to sleep. The pay is good, better'n good, even, and you're with a bunch of good guys, guys who feel the same way about a lot of things that most people don't even think about. What more do you need?"

Luke didn't answer. He sat up straight, then leaned forward to peer out the windshield between Marcelli and the still sleeping Junior. What he saw was anything but reassuring.

"We're here," Marcelli announced. "Wake up, Junior. We're here. Home, sweet home."

The car rocked to a halt in front of a low, Quonset-style building. Its tin roof and sides were over-thatched with branches hacked from nearby trees. Several others, equally camouflaged, stood in a rough semicircle behind it. A dozen vehicles, mostly jeeps, but including two olive-drab trucks and a baby-blue Continental, were parked under a thatched-roof, three-sided lean-to.

"Hit the bricks, gentlemen." Marcelli was expansive in his pronouncement, and Luke could see the man was getting pumped up, talking himself into an authority he knew he didn't possess.

They hopped out of the car, and Marcelli gave Junior the keys. "Put 'er away, would you, Junior? I want to introduce the new kids."

Luke looked around the camp, gawking in feigned awe. He took in as much as he could and immediately focused on the mixture of professionalism and playacting that had gone into it. He got the impression that some, if not most, of the men at the camp must have been playacting. It looked as much like kids playing war as it did real men competent with real weapons. The combination, unfortunately, was probably more deadly because it was so volatile and unpredictable.

"Come on, guys." Marcelli led the way to the main Quonset hut, obviously the command post for the camp.

Luke and Jake followed, lagging behind a few feet. Marcelli pushed into the hut, flinging back the mesh-reinforced screen door with a bang. It was dark inside, a single lamp all but swallowed by the gloom.

"Marshall, these are the new guys I told you about."

Akins was sitting behind a scarred metal desk. He didn't respond immediately, continuing to pore over some sheaves of computer paper spread out under the dim lamp. Marcelli shuffled uneasily, his feet rasping on the gritty planks of the floor.

"Maybe it's a bad time," Luke suggested.

At that, Akins dropped the last of the papers and shoveled them into a rough stack. He looked at Luke briefly, tamped the sheaf into a neat rectangle, and slipped it into an envelope. "I'll decide that, not you," he said.

Akins stood up and stepped around the corner of the desk. He walked deliberately, clasping his hands behind his back. The demeanor was that of every third-rate tyrant Luke had ever encountered, from the military, the police, even to the bureaucratic levels of government. Akins might have been a functionary at Motor Vehicle wanting to know why your previous license had been lost.

The leader of the Heartlanders planted himself in front of Luke. He cleared his throat. Never taking his eyes off Luke, he said, "Marcelli, I thought you were bringing one new man. That's what you told Andy."

"Yeah, well, unh, I thought . . ."

"Of course you did. Which one of these lames was the guy you told Andy about on the telephone?"

"Jake, unh, the big guy."

Still keeping his gaze locked on Luke, he continued the inquisition. "Then who is this?"

"Unh, that's Lou Simmons. He's Jake's friend and, unh, he wants to join too."

"What do you know about him?"

Luke was expecting Akins to check his teeth any second. Instead, he walked around behind Luke in a slow, stiff-legged strut. The next question came from behind Luke and was directed to him, rather than Marcelli. At the same instant Luke felt the unmistakable cold steel of a handgun muzzle, its small mouth yawning like the Grand Canyon. "Tell me about yourself, Mr. Simmons."

"I'm six feet two and my favorite Beatle was John."

Akins pressed the gun harder against the bone just below Luke's right ear. "Why are you here?"

"I'm beginning to wonder about that myself."

"You ever in the Army?"

"Sure."

"You know anything about discipline? Does the phrase 'bad attitude' mean anything to you, Mr. Simmons?"

"Not anymore."

"Why not?"

"I'm not in the Army now. A bad attitude is my prerogative as an American citizen."

The screen door grated on the threshold, and Akins turned, pulling the gun away. Luke rubbed the tender spot, feeling the circular impression with the tips of his fingers.

Junior stumbled into the dim interior.

"Junior," Akins snapped. "Take these men to Barracks Two. Get them some gear. Search their bags. And make sure they surrender any personal weapons."

"Yes, sir, Mr. Akins." Junior tossed a ragged salute and spun unsteadily on his heels. "Come on, you guys."

Akins raised his head and stared at Luke. "You got a lot of heart, Simmons," he said. "I like that. But I'm in charge here, understand? Remember it and we'll get along okay. Forget and I'll bury you."

Luke nodded. Without a word he stepped out after Junior. Jake followed, glaring over his shoulder at Akins. His fists were still clenched.

When they were gone, Akins turned his attention to Marcelli. "You asshole. You told Randall one guy, and you brought two. What do you know about them?"

"Just what I told you."

"You stay on them. We got a lot to do in the next couple of weeks. Anything goes wrong, I'll have your head, as well as theirs. I'm tired of covering your ass. You stick it out again, you better be wearing armor."

Marcelli nodded. "I'll watch 'em."

"You better."

CHAPTER 17

Junior led them to one of the huts in the semicircle behind the command post. They stepped inside, and the familiar smells brought a flood of sensations to both Jake and Luke. As much as you wanted to believe you'd left the service behind, a complex set of attitudes and memories was never far beneath the surface, like a second skeleton that wouldn't show on any X ray.

The place was deserted. It appeared that about half of the bunks had already been assigned.

"Take your pick, fellows. You can tell which ones are available. Blankets are in the footlockers for each bunk. There's a combination padlock in every empty locker."

Junior flopped down on one of the unclaimed bunks while they made their choices. For reasons of safety they opted not to take adjacent bunks. While they made up the beds, Junior prattled mindlessly, neither man paying him much attention.

When they had finished, Junior asked, "You guys carrying?"

"Not me," Luke said.

"Me, either," Jake volunteered.

"All right. I'll get you weapons issued, but you have to leave them in the armory except for training hours."

"Why's that?" Luke asked.

"Akins don't like weapons floating around. Too much can happen, you know?"

Luke grunted.

"Okay, I'll be back in a half hour. It'll be time for chow. I'll introduce you around."

"Thanks, Junior." Jake smiled. "See you then. Oh, by the way, how *is* the chow?"

Junior slapped his thick middle. "It ain't great, but there's plenty of it." He laughed and stood to leave. "Listen," he said, almost as an afterthought, "Akins can be a mean son of a bitch until he knows you. Don't take nothing personally. Just do like he says and you'll get along fine."

"Thanks for the tip. But it's a little late for that," Luke said.

"Yeah, I guess it is, ain't it? See you."

When Junior had gone, Luke gestured to Jake to come close, then whispered, "I think this place might be bugged. Let's assume it is."

"Got it."

Jake went to his footlocker, rummaged around for the small travel shaving kit he'd brought along, and zipped it open. He palmed a small disk and slipped it into his shirt. Rezipping the kit, he said, "I think I'll go take a look around. You want to come?"

"Nope. I think I'll just tidy up here a bit. Too damn much dirt to suit me."

"You always were a fussy bastard. See you at chow."

Jake was gone. Luke examined the barracks with a practiced eye. All the requisite features were evident. Playmates of the month adorned the doors of several lockers, and one centerfold, from a down-scale skin magazine, was stapled to the ceiling over a bunk. The place smelled of sweat and shoe polish, leather and insect repellent. The windows, Luke noted, were meshed with heavy steel, and he crossed the floor to take a good look at one. The mesh was welded to a heavy steel frame bolted into the window frame at all four corners. It looked more appropriate for a stockade than a barracks.

He walked through a door at one end. A smaller room, as Spartan in its decor, contained the latrines and a communal shower. The half dozen shower heads were beginning to rust, and some were covered with a thin, greenish-gray patina. The place was clean but still had that heavy scent of hard use and strong soap. Whatever else Akins was, he certainly was an able administrator. It was obvious that discipline was demanded and enforced. There was no indication of laxity or halfhearted homage to military rules and regs. They were here and they were working.

Luke stepped outside, into brilliant sunlight. The air was still, and so far the camp was quiet. The day had begun more than two hours ago for most of the camp's inhabitants, but they were nowhere to be seen. A piercing whistle caught his attention. He spotted Jake lounging against the base of a tree at the edge of the clearing.

"We got a bit of a problem, Luke," he whispered.

"What's up?"

"There's no way we'll ever be able to get to a phone without one of these geeks along. The transmitter let Ben track us here, but we're still badly outnumbered. Junior tells me there's at least forty men in this little battalion."

"We got a bigger problem than that, Jake."

"Talk to me."

"Akins is the man we want to watch. How do we do it? He's the boss. If he tells us to go into the swamp and catch frogs, what choice do we have? How do we keep tabs on him?"

"Already figured that one out, lad. All we have to do is figure out how old Marshall gets around. My money's on the Lincoln, what do you think?"

"No argument there."

"So all we have to do is stick another transmitter on the car. Ben will figure it out. He already knows the location of the camp, so it shouldn't be a problem."

"You mean we can take care of ourselves here, right?"

"You got it."

"Let's do it."

"First chance I get. Probably tonight. As long as Akins hangs around overnight, it's a piece of cake."

*   *   *

Jake lay on the bunk, his eyes closed, waiting for the horseplay to simmer down. The rest of the men had come in late that evening, stinking of swamp water and bitching about bugs. The mess hall had smelled like a primeval bog. The men were too tired to say much, and most had ignored the newcomers altogether. Those who were inclined to be more sociable had nodded hello but little more.

Once they'd hit the barracks, things had loosened up a bit, but most of them were still quiet. It wasn't until they got out of the shower and felt a little more like human beings and a little less like pre-hominid experiments that they began to chatter. There was an easy camaraderie among those who knew one another. They formed a united front against the new arrivals. One man, a big, red-necked Oklahoman named Orville Hobbs, seemed to be the unofficial leader of the barracks.

Hobbs had thrown his weight around a bit, making Jake change bunks twice and complaining about the poor shine on Jake's combat boots. Luke recognized the phenomenon for what it was. Gorillas did it, so did elk. Lions did it, and house cats did it too. But nobody did it better than man.

Orville Hobbs was cock of the walk, and he'd be damned if he was going to relinquish that title easily.

Luke had watched the big Oklahoman run his number on Jake. O'Bannion was no pussycat, but he was sensitive to their delicate predicament. Rather than risk a confrontation, Jake was willing to swallow his pride and take some abuse. And Hobbs was no pushover. Big-boned and thickly muscled, he outweighed Jake by nearly twenty pounds, and he was at least ten years younger. Luke was thankful he didn't have to lay money on the outcome of what looked to be a fairly even match.

When Hobbs had satisfied himself that Jake was no threat, he turned his attentions to Luke. Luke, too, was willing to compromise, but there was a point beyond which he would not be pushed. The big Okie seemed to sense it. His challenge to Luke was only tentative, and when Luke ignored it, Hobbs let it drop, as if in asserting his dominance over Jake, Luke had been subdued as well.

The tight ring of eager observers had quickly broken up into small groups of card players, checkers fanatics, and a couple of solitary readers. Luke hung around the fringes of a spirited game of stud poker, while Jake tried to blend into the background. Dead tired from the morning's maneuvers, most of the guys hit the hay early.

It was exactly what Jake had been counting on. Now, all the lights but one extinguished, Jake rolled restlessly, unused to the stiff support of a military bunk. The mattress rustled noisily with every toss and turn.

Finally the small, battery-powered reading lamp went out. Jake heard the thud of a paperback on the thick planking of the barracks floor. He slipped a hand into the breast pocket of his pajamas, making certain the small transmitter was still there. The size of a dime and not much thicker, it had a range of ten miles. The small battery would keep it going for six months or more. It was as good as they came, and as long as the guy on the other end was diligent, it was all you needed to keep track of anything from a moose to a naval task force. Ben was reliable, so there was no worry on that score.

When every breath seemed deep and regular, all the men asleep but himself, Jake rose quietly. On bare feet, he moved to the latrine. A small pocket flash confirmed what he thought he had remembered—there was no way out that end of the building. He'd have to chance leaving by the front door.

Unfamiliar with the camp's security measures, he had no idea whether a guard was posted, and if so, where. Common sense suggested a guard was unnecessary, but the military obsession of Marshall Akins was no slave of logic. Jake would have to assume there was at least one.

Once outside, Jake stopped to get his bearings. In the dim light he could see the blue Lincoln under the thatched roof. Strolling casually, he popped a piece of bubble gum in his mouth and chewed vigorously. He worked the gum into a pliable state, then blew a bubble to see how sticky it was.

The bubble burst, leaving stringy tentacles stuck to his nose and chin. He peeled the gum loose and popped it back in, chewing more slowly now. When the gum was thoroughly chewed, Jake drifted off to one side of the lean-to, taking care not to seem overly concerned whether or not he was observed.

At the corner of the lean-to he stood, hands in pockets, watching the sky. He slapped idly at a mosquito on his neck and cursed softly for the benefit of anyone who might be listening. So far he hadn't seen or heard a soul. Slipping quickly into the lean-to, he took the gum out of his mouth and wadded it around the transmitter. Standing behind the car, he searched with his fingertips, still standing tall. When he found what he was looking for, he jammed the sticky gum in behind the rear license plate, tamping it firmy around the mounting screw.

Jake slipped back away from the lean-to and whistled softly, the very picture of a bored man on a midnight stroll.

If things went as expected, the coming days would be anything but boring.

CHAPTER 18

Marshall Akins paced back and forth in front of the men. The sky was already an achingly bright yellow. It was going to be the hottest day yet. The wordless pace seemed studied, an artistic gesture rather than a nervous habit. It seemed to Luke that Akins had studied George C. Scott as Patton and consciously aped the stylized portrait.

Finally he spoke. "This is it. This is our last milk run. You get it right today, or you don't get it. In case you're wondering what I mean, let me show you."

Akins held his hands out, palms up. Pete Marcelli detached himself from the cluster of noncoms standing to one side, apart from the rank and file. He yanked an M16 from its stack, and, in a ragged strut that unconsciously parodied that of Akins, approached the latter and slapped the rifle into the outstretched hands.

Akins hefted the weapon, checked its action, then turned casually, brought the carbine to his waist, and squeezed the trigger. The burst was expected. The shattering windshield of a jeep parked to the right was not.

The men murmured, and Akins interrupted them, like a high-school senior telling freshmen of his sexual conquests. "That's right . . . live ammo. All of it. You guys are going

121

to be out there with live ammo. The target series is familiar to you, but this time it's the real thing. An observer will be at every target. After you nail it, assuming you do, wait there until he checks you off his list, then move on to the next. At the end of the run you'll be told where to wait until the last man comes in. And I mean last. Nobody is dismissed until you all complete the course. Keep that in mind out there. Now let's hump it, fellows.''

Akins marched away theatrically, his feet squishing on the soggy, weed-littered ground. Luke watched him in disbelief. It was a masterstroke of theater, he thought. Theater of the Absurd. Akins was sending a bunch of half-assed soldiers into the swamp with live ammo. If they didn't cut each other to pieces, it would be a miracle.

Standing in line to be issued his weapon, Luke wondered what was coming. This "graduation" exercise was obviously a prelude to something. Something big.

Luke imagined the beeping bug in Akins's car and hoped like hell that Ben was in range. Like his own beating heart, the electronic pulse was steady and silent. He was feeling more like a hostage than a penetrator. It was a feeling he wasn't used to, and one he didn't like.

When he received his own M16, he pushed off with a shout, like those before him. In his own ears it sounded hollow and false, but then so did the shouts of the others. It was as if they, too, were going through the motions for some purpose they either didn't understand or feared.

Once in the forest, Luke concentrated on the task at hand. Forty men, each armed with an M16, were going to be roaming around in the wilderness, each trying to be the first man in and, most likely, nervous as hell. It would take all his wits to avoid getting shot accidentally. Jake had been behind him in line, and he looked for a place to wait. If they worked as a team, they would have a better chance.

Concealing himself in a small knot of vine-draped undergrowth, he watched several men work their way past. He had chosen a spot that gave him a good view of the least tangled area, not exactly a path, but the line of least resistance. Most, if not all, of the men were certain to take that route.

One by one they filed through, some running in a crouch, others walking upright, their weapons cradled loosely in crooked arms. They looked like nothing so much as kids playing cowboys and Indians.

The next one through should be Jake. He peered up the path, waiting for O'Bannion. A snapping twig behind him caused him to whirl. Jake stood on the other side of the knot, a huge grin on his face.

He dropped to his knees and wormed through the clinging vines. "I figured I might as well get some real practice in. This Mickey Mouse shit is getting old real fast."

"This Mickey Mouse shit might get us shot if we're not careful. I can't believe Akins is doing something this stupid."

"He must have a big deal up his sleeve. Got any ideas?"

"Nope. Did you get the bug on Akins's car?"

"Yeah. It was close, but I managed. We'll be okay if he doesn't sweep it."

"I hope to God Ben is close enough to pick him up."

"We're in deep shit if he isn't."

"I guess we might as well get on with this ridiculous exercise."

"Right-o, boss. You take the point, oh, fearless leader."

Luke scowled good-naturedly. Jake's humor had been a godsend more than once. He hoped it still worked. Climbing slowly out of concealment, he spotted the next man moving slowly through a thin stand of trees. Swiveling his head back and forth, he looked as if he thought the targets were live things that could shoot back at him. It was just that attitude that worried Luke. A sudden twig snapping underfoot might be enough to send the guy over the edge. More than a few of the men, he knew, were combat veterans, and the possibility of reversion to old habits was very real.

Luke froze in his tracks. Jake slipped in behind him. "That's Jackson," he whispered. "He was the last man. If we let him go by, we should be in pretty good shape. We can just watch our front and make it through without getting shot."

"Yeah, maybe. But some of these clowns are likely to walk in circles."

While they waited for Jackson to nervously work his way past, Luke spotted a shadowy figure behind him.

"I thought you said Jackson was the last man, Jake."

"He was, why?"

"Look, about thirty yards behind him."

Luke pointed with his left hand. The shadowy figure was keeping up with Jackson, neither gaining nor losing ground, constantly adjusting its pace to the stuttering progress of the nervous man. Luke could see beads of sweat on Jackson's forehead.

"Christ Almighty," Jake exploded. "That's Sanchez! What the hell is he doing here?"

The two men watched as Jackson made his way awkwardly through the undergrowth. The shadowy figure behind him, now indisputably Ben Sanchez, mirrored his progress with a fluid grace that was everything Jackson's wasn't. They held their breath as Jackson came within five yards of them. He was so busy checking the trees, stabbing this way and that with his nervous gaze, that he never even looked at their place of concealment. A moment later he was gone. They could hear his unsteady progress, breaking twigs and swishing through heavily leaved undergrowth, for several minutes after he had gone out of sight.

Ben, now relaxed in the manner of a man on a leisurely stroll in the woods, made right for them. He dropped down to his knees as casually as if he were a few minutes late for a picnic.

"How the hell did you know where we were?" Jake whispered.

"White eyes leave sign."

"Cut the cigar-store Indian crap," Jake snapped. He was annoyed that Ben had found them so easily.

"What are you doing here?" Luke asked.

"I followed you guys, just like we planned. When I got close, I figured I might as well come on in and take a look around. That's some setup."

"Yeah, it is, but these guys are something else. They don't have a clue."

"That's why they're dangerous," Ben suggested. "They

have some combat expertise. They might be rusty, but they've been there. And the reason they're here is that they miss the rush. They're flaky and unpredictable.''

"How do you know that?" Jake demanded. "You didn't see much of them.''

"I don't have to see very much to know that. It's in their faces. Jackson, there, the guy I was following, is probably typical, anyway. I was in the bushes across from the clearing when Akins sent him out. He was raring to go. Don't think he's a drugstore cowboy. You'd be surprised how quickly it will all come back.''

"What makes you say that?"

"I know the type. Hell, I *am* the type." Ben looked off at the forest, as if he were imagining some other trees in some other country. Luke knew where. He waited patiently for Ben to come back.

"I got two blips on the screen. Where'd you put the other bug?''

"Akins's car. I want to keep tabs on him," Luke said. "Follow him wherever he goes."

"How do I get in touch with you?"

"You don't. Use Tran as a drop. Call him with whatever you pick up. We'll check in with him when we can.''

"That won't be easy."

"Tell me about it."

"I guess I better get going. Have fun." Ben smiled. "And, Jake, don't shoot yourself in the foot, okay?''

They watched the Apache move off so noiselessly, they might have been watching a silent film. With a final thrust into a clump of bushes he was gone. Not even the leaves betrayed his passage.

"I guess we better hit it," Luke said. "I'll bet my last dollar Akins has something special in mind for us. I think he's waiting for us to fuck up."

"I hope he holds his breath," Jake said.

They checked the map once more, for the sequence of targets, then moved out. In quick succession they scored on each one, checked in with the monitors, and moved on to the next. The woods reverberated with the sound of automatic weapons.

Much of the firing sounded aimless, as if the men were shooting at anything that moved. Each target, well concealed and ingeniously rigged, would spring out of concealment, under the control of its monitor. Failure to hit it in five seconds was considered a death warrant. Those who failed were pulled at that point and sent on to the main staging area.

As the men from Deadly Force worked their way through the course, the volume of fire gradually abated. Some men had reached the end of the course, but Luke knew that in all probability at least as many had been "killed" and sent on ahead in disgrace.

They had three targets to go when Luke spotted something out of the corner of his eye. He grabbed Jake by the shoulder and pulled him down. Pointing toward a clump of bushes, he motioned for Jake to follow him. He wormed his way on his stomach, taking care to slide under the thickest tangled vines, and maneuvered around small stands of shrubbery.

Four men stood in a small clearing. One of them was Marshall Akins. Peter Marcelli and Junior Riley were also there. Luke didn't recognize the fourth man. Akins was livid. As they slid closer, they could hear him snarling.

"Marcelli, I warned you a hundred times not to go off on your own."

"I swear to God, Mr. Akins, I don't know what you're talking about."

"I'm talking about the bank job in Ferris, Arkansas. And what happened to Ralph Perkins?"

"I already told you. He said he wanted to go home. He was tired of playin' soldier, he said."

"Then why isn't he home? Why can't anyone find him?"

"How should I know?"

"Because you killed him? You killed him and you hid the money. It was you guys who knocked over the bank."

"No way, man. I wouldn't do that."

"Junior, what do you have to say about it?"

"It's like Pete said. Honest to God, Ralph didn't want to be

here no more. He said he was going home. Maybe he just
wanted to get out. Maybe he didn't go home."

"Did you know they found his body? Yesterday?"

"No, sir. Why would I know that?"

"Did you know he was killed with an M16? One of our
M16s, one of the guns you were supposed to drop at the
farm?"

"No, sir. I didn't know that."

"Who shot him, you or Marcelli?"

"I don't know what you're talking about."

"Junior, let me tell you something. I don't blame you.
You're nothing but a follower. It had to be Marcelli, here.
Had to be. Isn't that right?"

"Yes, sir."

"And some of you are trying to undermine me. Some
of you are reporting on our activities to the federal government. I think Pete Marcelli is one of those who are trying to
undo all the work I've been trying to do. How can I save
this country from its worst instincts if I can't trust my own
people?"

"Yes, sir, I understand."

"The Jews and the Communists want to take our land and
give it to people who shouldn't even be here, people who are
no better than Stone Age savages, bleeding the country dry
with welfare and drugs and crime. An honest man doesn't
stand a chance anymore, Junior. I want to do something
about that. And Pete Marcelli, and others like him, don't
want me to. Pete Marcelli is Judas, Junior. But he won't get
the chance to kiss me in front of the high priest."

"No, sir. I understand what you mean."

"So I'll tell you what I'm going to do. I'm going to let you
walk on this. But there's one thing you have to do first."

"Yes, sir?"

"Is it a deal?"

"Yes, sir." Junior was trembling. His voice quavered
noticeably. His hands were shaking. "It's a deal."

"Don't let him talk you into nothing, Junior. He don't
know what he's talking about. We didn't do anything."

Junior looked at Marcelli but said nothing.

Marcelli continued. "He's going to try to use you, just like he uses everybody else. Don't let him do it."

"Are you ready, Junior?" Akins asked.

"Yes, sir."

"Good. Here you are." Akins handed Junior Marcelli's M16.

Junior looked confused. He looked at the rifle, then at Akins. "What's this for?"

"Why, to complete your half of the bargain, naturally. It is the instrument by which the Judas shall be removed from our midst, before he can do any more harm."

"What do you mean?"

"Mr. Marcelli betrayed me. He betrayed you, all of us. He doesn't deserve to live."

"You mean, shoot him?"

"Very good, Junior. You're smarter than I thought. Certainly smarter than Mr. Marcelli gave you credit for."

"I can't do that, Mr. Akins."

"But you have to, Junior. You have to do it. Because if you don't, Mr. Robinson, here, will have to shoot you both. One death is certainly preferable to two, don't you think? Especially if it's not yours?"

"Yes, sir."

Junior raised the weapon, pointing it almost casually at Marcelli's midsection.

Jake tensed, ready to make a move. Luke grabbed his arm. "Hold it, Jake. We can't—"

"But we can't stand here and watch this. At least, I can't. . . ."

"We don't have any choice, Jake. How long do you think Akins would let us live? He's not too sure about us as it is. If we interfere, he'll kill us both. We're not ready to start a war over this."

Junior raised the carbine a little higher. His finger trembled in the trigger guard. The crack was swift and gone almost before anyone heard it. Junior's M16 was aimed at the ground. Marcelli, realizing his last chance, made a run for the trees. But Robinson was faster. He raised his own rifle and fired a burst at the fleeing man.

Luke saw the impact of the slugs, a ragged line of bright red splotches replacing the rumpled cloth almost instantaneously.

CHAPTER 19

James Alfred Robinson, Jimbo to his friends, of which there were few, lay sleeping. A dank sweat soaked his sheets, seeping into the stiff mattress beneath him. A night of heavy drinking, not as uncommon as his friends would like, and all too common for those who didn't like him at all, had had the usual effect. The leaves outside Barracks One rustled slightly. There was a breeze, but not enough to cool things off.

The first patter of rain on the tin roof sounded like slapping fingertips. A damp fog rolled among the trees surrounding the camp, moving in discrete clouds, like moist wraiths, snagging on vines and thorny branches, ripping apart, then re-forming in a mutable panorama.

The hinges creaked, and Jimbo turned over with a groan. He started, sat half up as if he'd heard the soft squeal, then fell back to sleep with a damp thud. The resistant metal argued against moving farther, but the figure on the threshold was patient, moving the door inches at a time, stopping each time the rusted metal protested.

When it had been pulled halfway, the figure slipped inside, its bare feet whispering on the gritty floor. Stopping, waiting for its eyes to adjust to the interior darkness, the shadowy blur reached out with one hand to grab the foot of the first bunk.

Feeling its way, it found the third, kicked a boot, and held its breath as the heavy leather scraped on the wood, then fell over with a sharp thud. A flurry of sibilant motion subsided almost immediately as the fitful sleepers reacted to the sound. The shadow moved again, this time sliding silently along the third bunk.

A snarl of insects, driven by the rain, raked the screen, their wings scraping against the metal like a thousand tiny rasps. Jimbo began to talk to himself, rolling his head from side to side. The man standing over his bed couldn't see him in the dark, but imagined the unsightly strands of drunken drool staining the pillowcase a light amber. It was one of the things about Jimbo he liked least.

The man took a deep breath, expanding his lungs and holding the air in until the bright stars of approaching unconsciousness flashed behind his closed lids. Shaking his head, still uncertain of himself and still questioning his own motives, he stared down at the dim bulk on the Spartan mattress. There were too many contradictions, too many conflicting emotions. He knelt on one knee, resting his left hand on the edge of the bed. It wasn't exactly an attitude of prayer, but he realized it was as close as he was ever likely to come.

A flash of silent lightning splashed brittle illumination around the room, its intensity washing out color and painting the room in shadow and bleached tones, a still life in charcoal and pastels. The man cocked his ear for the distant roll of thunder, but all he heard were the insects clawing at the screen.

The man knew further delay was pointless. Some things would never change, no matter how long you waited. He hunched closer, still on one knee, and moved toward the head of the bed. The mattress, stiff under his left hand, creaked on its springs. He could see the piglike face now, turned toward him in the dim light. One eye was half open, as if the sleeping man had been playing a game with him. He reached out with his right hand and passed it quickly across Jimbo's face, but the eye never blinked.

The man placed his left hand over Jimbo's mouth. With a deft flick of the right, once and then again, he did what he had come to do. The sticky burbling of escaping air, followed by a slight tremor and one violent spasm, told him he had accomplished his task. He held the hand clamped tightly across the slack jaw for several minutes. The blade in his other hand was still buried in flesh.

Reluctantly he relaxed the tension of his grasp, feeling with his fingertips for any movement. There was none, and no sound. Even the burbling had ceased. The bugs continued to rasp against the wire screen. The man stood up slowly, still holding on to Jimbo's slack jaw, as if reluctant to break contact. Like a departing lover at a frenzied train station, he saw nothing but Jimbo, the one eye still open, but glazed now as it had never been.

"That was for Pete Marcelli," he whispered.

The shouting woke Luke with a start. He jumped up and ran to the door of Barracks Two. Jake was already outside, and several of their barracks mates were sprinting across the compound to the door of Barracks One. Luke ran out into the fine rain, his bare feet splashing in the ground water. At the door to Barracks One, a knot of men had crammed onto the porch.

The men were all talking at once, and Luke couldn't get a sense of what had happened. Jake was in the center of the knot and used his bulk to push on through and into the barracks.

Marshall Akins, wearing only jeans and moccasins, raced up to Luke. "What's going on? What the hell is all the shouting about?"

"I don't know, I just got here. Let's see if we can't get inside."

"Step aside there, you men. Get the hell out of the way. Let us through."

The men shoved and pushed, expanding and contracting like a swarm of bees as they tried to get out of Akins's way. Finally a narrow gap appeared, and Akins pushed on through, Luke right behind him.

Jake was kneeling beside a bunk halfway into the barracks. A cluster of men obscured whatever he was doing. Akins grabbed one of the onlookers by the collar and yanked him roughly away. Luke was surprised at the man's strength.

"Stand back, you men. Let me in there."

The small crowd backed away, and Luke was able to push in beside Akins.

The body on the bunk had bled an impossible volume, and the thick, clotted sheets around the neck and shoulders gave off a sweetish odor, like rotting fruit. Luke didn't need to get any closer to know that the man was dead.

"Christ Almighty," Akins muttered. "Jimbo. What the fuck happened?"

"Somebody cut his throat. Twice." Jake said. The matter-of-fact tone to his voice was meaningful only to Luke.

"I can see that. But who did it? And why?"

"I expect you'd have a better idea than we would, Mr. Akins," Jake said.

"What do you mean? Are you accusing me of this monstrous act?"

"Not at all. It's just that you know him better than I do. If anybody would have some clue as to what prompted his murder, I think it would be you."

"I have no idea." Akins's voice quavered slightly. His features were stiff and pale, as if painted with a chalky glaze that immobilized them. He kept staring at the dead man, his fingers alternately reaching out and twitching closed into a loose fist.

"Why don't we get everyone out of here?" Luke suggested. He noticed dozens of ants already beginning to scurry over the bloody sheets and skitter across Jimbo's cheeks and forehead.

"All right," Akins shouted. "You heard the man. Clear out! All of you."

The men grumbled but started to shuffle backward, almost relieved to be getting away from the gruesome sight. Luke heard one of them mutter, "Son of a bitch, I wish I'da done it. Motherfucker had it coming. Whoever it was ought to get a medal."

By the time Luke turned around, the man had finished speaking. He noted the faces, most of which were unfamiliar. He couldn't help noticing they seemed more curious than horrified, as if they all shared the speaker's sentiments.

When the men had gone, Akins turned to Luke. "I don't suppose you have any idea what caused this."

"Sorry, I don't. I think Jake has a point, though. What reason would anyone have? You know the men better than anyone else. And you knew Jimbo better too. He didn't have any close friends here, that much I already know. Other than that, I don't have a clue. I gather he wasn't too popular."

"No, he wasn't. The men resented him, I think. He was a good soldier and followed orders."

"That doesn't usually get your throat cut for you," Jake pointed out. "There has to be some other reason."

Akins ignored him. He waved his hands in the air, like a stringless puppet ready to crumple. Luke was struck by how different a figure Akins had cut the previous afternoon, when he'd played judge and jury for Pete Marcelli. There was no doubt in Luke's mind that whoever had murdered Jimbo had done so in retaliation for the brutal execution.

The most likely candidate would be Junior Riley, but it seemed too cold and calculated a thing, more like a long, simmering vengeance brought to fruition than a swift retaliation. Luke doubted Junior capable of so abrupt and decisive a move. That Junior might be able to kill a man in cold blood seemed questionable. In the heat of anger, perhaps, but the time for that had been yesterday afternoon, not in the dead of night. And not with a knife. The choice of weapon, as Luke well knew, often told you more about the killer than any other single thing.

Akins sat down on the next bunk. "We have to get him out of here. And we have to keep it quiet. If this leaks out, I'm finished. We'll have to dump him in the swamp somewhere. Simmons, get a couple of men in here and take care of it, will you? I don't want him found. Ever."

"You got any suggestions?"

"I don't care, just do it. Get him out of here." Akins stood and walked toward the window. He was already getting over the shock. Luke was worried about Junior Riley. He knew Akins would immediately seize on Marcelli's young friend as the most likely assassin. Somehow he had to steer Akins away. "Why don't you go back to your office, let me and Jake handle this. We'll find out who did it."

Suddenly in command again, Akins snapped, "You better."

CHAPTER 20

"What the hell are we going to do about this?" Jake asked when Akins had left the barracks. "Jesus, I think I'm gonna be sick."

"There's nothing we can do, Jake. You know that. We've got bigger fish to fry, and nothing we do is going to make any difference to Jimbo."

"Don't remind me."

"I guess we might as well get started, then."

"Christ, the guy must have relatives someplace, don't you think? They ought to be told about this."

"Not now. Not until we find out what Akins is up to. And not until we recover those weapons."

"I guess you're right, Luke. But I don't like it, all the same."

"You think I do? Come on, give me a hand here." Luke began to yank the sheet out from under the mattress. Jake grabbed the other side, struggling to keep his nausea under control.

"Whoever did this really knew what he was doing," Luke said. "It's a neat job."

"I've seen a lot of things in my time. Lots worse than this, really. Including a lot of dead people who didn't deserve to die. But this is so damn cold-blooded. I can't explain it, but—"

"Jake, forget about it. Let's just get him out of here."

Jake bent, grabbed one end of the bizarre package, and staggered back through the door. Luke waddled after him, cradling the other end in his arms. Jake climbed backward into a jeep, nearly losing his balance as he negotiated the awkward step over the driveshaft hump. He stepped down off the far side of the jeep, and together he and Luke lowered the dead man into the rear.

Jake climbed into the driver's seat, then waited for Luke to walk around behind the vehicle and climb into the passenger side.

"Where to?"

"I don't know. One place is as good as another, I guess. What about that sinkhole we saw yesterday?"

"You got it."

Jake kicked the jeep into gear, fumbling with the clutch and bucking across the clearing. He steered for a narrow gap in the trees, and the jeep just managed to squeeze through, branches whipping at the windshield. Luke scratched one arm badly on some thorns and wiped the blood away with a handkerchief.

"What do we do when we find the sinkhole, Luke?"

"Pray."

When they got back to the compound an hour later, Jake returned the jeep to its parking place under the lean-to, while Luke headed for Akins's office. He'd just earned a little credit with the quixotic leader, and wanted to make sure Akins recorded it in his ledger.

The blue Continental, parked alongside Akins's Quonset hut when they'd left, was gone. Luke stood on the wooden deck outside the door and knocked. After several seconds with no answer, he rapped more sharply on the screen door, causing its wooden frame to bounce against the doorjamb. When there was still no answer, Luke slipped inside, glancing over his shoulder to see whether anyone was watching.

Inside, he stepped quickly to the window and peered out into the clearing without moving the curtains aside. He couldn't see the entire clearing, but it seemed deserted. He walked into the inner office, thinking that perhaps Akins had fallen asleep, but the room was deserted. In Akins's sleeping quarters, the bed was neatly made, its crisp hospital corners snug and geometrically perfect. Akins was one stickler who didn't exempt himself from the rigors of his regulations. Luke was more than a little surprised. It suggested discipline but implied even more: Akins was a perfectionist.

A compulsive personality, he probably had a journal or a diary somewhere, using it to record everything that happened at the camp, perhaps even away from it. Keeping one ear on the outer door, Luke stepped to the desk and sat down in the straight-backed leather chair behind it.

The center drawer of the desk was locked, as Luke suspected. He grabbed a letter opener and slid it up against the lock. Exerting a steady pressure to the side, he felt the latch begin to give then; with a snap and a click it was all the way open. Luke listened for a moment, then opened the drawer.

He fumbled in the rear of the drawer, keeping his eyes on the doorway. He felt a thick book, bound in pebbled cloth, probably a simulated leather. Pulling the book to the front of the drawer, he opened it without taking it out of the desk. It wasn't a diary. Instead, he found himself staring at lists of names, arranged in double columns. Page after page, followed in each case by a second column of numbers. There were no dollar signs, but each number ended in two decimal places, and Luke was convinced it had to be some sort of financial record.

Flipping through the pages quickly, he kept his eye peeled for a familiar name but found none. The entries occupied more than thirty pages. As far as he could tell, none of the names appeared more than once.

He thought for a second about stealing the book but realized that the risk was too great. He didn't have a prayer of getting the ledger out of the office and securely hidden without being seen. At night, perhaps, but Akins slept in the next room and would surely hear him. He found himself hoping Akins failed to return later that day. Pinning his hopes on that possibility, Luke quickly surveyed the rest of the desk drawers, then jimmied a file cabinet.

Rapidly scanning the contents of each drawer, he made mental notes of the location of promising-looking documents. Somewhere in the welter of paper and almost obsessive records, he hoped, was the single piece of evidence they needed to bring to a screeching halt the whole elaborate machine Akins had so carefully assembled. And if, as seemed almost certain, Akins was behind the rifling of the Ozark Armory, the proof was probably right here in this small room. All Luke had to do was find it.

Reclosing the drawers and returning, as best he could, each thing to its proper place, Luke decided he had to get copies of anything and everything. He would return that night, if possible, with the microfilm camera.

Tyler Hamilton dropped his binoculars. They slapped his chest with something like the sound of a guillotine striking home. He ground a butt out underfoot and turned to his companion.

"I don't know who those new guys are, but you better see what you can find out."

"Tyler, I don't know what you're worrying about. Marcelli vouched for them."

"And where is Marcelli now?"

"So, he got a little out of hand. It happens."

"Andy, Andy . . . how many times have I told you? Stealing petty cash is getting out of hand. Running amok and jeopardizing everything we've all worked for for so long is more than high spirits. It's deadly idiocy. You might not mind taking a fall on this, but I'll be damned if I will. Look, even if I were an admirer of Akins, which I'm not, I'd have my doubts. But he thinks he's the second coming of Napoleon. He wants to be emperor, though only God knows of what. It's got to stop."

"What can you do about it.? You want him taken out, then let me take him out. Why not be done with it?"

"No, no. He's still useful for a little while yet. There is a good deal we can extract out of him before we cut our losses.''

"I'm not so sure I like the way you say that, Tyler."

"What do you mean? What the hell are you all so damn worried about? Things are manageable. We've had a few rough spots, we'll get over them. My friends and I are very capable and, lest you forget, not a little influential."

"Yeah, yeah. Sing it again and I'll dance to it. I know it by heart. But so far you've fucked up as least as often as Akins. And that isn't even what worries me. What worries me is when I might suddenly be a tool to be used and thrown away, just like Akins."

"Don't be ridiculous, man. Akins is an egomaniac. He won't listen to reason, and he won't follow orders. Are you like that? Do you have trouble listening to instructions?"

"No. But then, Marshall never did, either. Not until you guys started changing the rules on him. How the hell is anybody supposed to know how to play the game when the rule book gets rewritten every damn day?"

"Stop exaggerating. And stop bellyaching . . . you're beginning to get on my nerves."

"Like Marshall?"

Tyler Hamilton heard the rasp almost at once. He froze an instant, not sure whether to react or to pretend he hadn't heard a thing. He couldn't afford to let Randall see how nervous he was. Finally, after what seemed suitably long to establish the ice water in his veins, he turned his head, keeping his body rigid.

The muzzle of the .45 seemed larger than he remembered. Nestled securely in Randall's tanned fist, it didn't waver at all. Hamilton noticed the knuckles on Randall's hand. They were the same brown color as the back of his hand. He was squeezing the gun tightly. Either Randall was not intending to use the weapon, or he was not at all disturbed at the prospect of blowing him away.

Hamilton sighed deeply. His left hand inched across his chest, the fingertips fumbling with his lapel before sliding underneath it.

"Do it and you'll never see Brooks Brothers again, Hamilton. I guarantee it."

"I think we'll have to talk about this sometime soon, Andy."

"I've said all I'm gonna say. You just walk away. This time. I see you again, they'll need a week to find all that's left of you."

Hamilton let his hand drop to his side. A moment later Randall was gone. Hamilton yanked a half-empty pack of cigarettes from his pocket. His hands shook. When he finally extracted a butt, it snapped in his fingers. The next one survived to reach his mouth, but lighting it was an adventure.

It was definitely time to wrap things up. In as neat and small a package as he could manage. This time there would be no loose ends.

CHAPTER 21

Luke slipped out of the barracks with his heart pounding. Akins had still not returned, but to preserve his image, he had suggested a rotating guard, and Luke was now trying to defeat the very safeguard he had himself installed. The screen door slipped out of his grasp, but he caught it before it slapped home. He had to get the pictures. Akins had returned that morning, then left abruptly, but the rumor was that he would be returning again the following day.

Ben had the assignment of tailing Akins. Once he left, there was nobody to transfer the film to Tran Cao, waiting expectantly in Phoenix. Ben made arrangements for Calvin Steeples to fly in, but getting the film to him wasn't going to be easy.

The forest was deathly still. Even the bugs seemed to have been cowed by two days of rain. The guard would be sitting at a small table just outside the command post, and Luke had to slip around behind the barracks. Once he had it between himself and the guard, he could relax. There was no moon, but the sky was crystal-clear, and the stars, unmuzzled from two days of solid clouds, seemed to sparkle with extraordinary intensity. Luke thought he might have been able to see even in the shadows.

He hit the edge of the trees without mishap. From here it was just a matter of good timing. Everything had been going wrong on this assignment, and Luke felt he was due for a change of luck. A hundred yards into the trees, he heard a soft whistle. As agreed, he stood still and waited, dropping down to keep his silhouette below the undergrowth. He shivered when he realized that whoever had killed Jimbo had been moving about at this time of night and could very well be out here in the forest with him.

The hand on his shoulder was reassuring. Calvin squatted beside him. "You got it?"

"Yeah, here. Two rolls. Tell Tran to pay particular attention to the maps. I don't know what city they represent, but they're pretty detailed, and there are some ID numbers in one corner. He might be able to use them."

"What's happening?"

"Akins is getting ready to make a move. I don't have a clue what it is, but I'm sure those maps are connected. Ben's on his tail."

"Anything else?"

"No, what about you?"

"Well, we've narrowed Akins's army connection down to about two dozen possibilities. I don't think we can take it much further than that unless we catch a break."

"You watching them?"

"No way. Not possible. I talked to Colonel Milford, but he says General Wilson won't authorize any surveillance. Can't spare the personnel, he says."

"Christ, you didn't tell Wilson who the suspects are, did you?"

"Of course not. I don't trust Wilson, and I'm not entirely sure I trust Milford, either. That guy gives me the creeps."

"All right, stay on it. There's a long list of names in a ledger I copied. Maybe there's a connection there." Luke drew a thick envelope out of his shirt after undoing three buttons. He handed it to Calvin.

"Christ, this is heavy. What is it?"

"It's a photocopy of some computer lists I found in Akins's

desk. I don't know what it's for, but Tran might be able to figure something out.''

"How the hell did you get the copy, tell Akins you were going to town to duplicate some of his papers?''

"Not hardly. He's got one of those desktop copiers in his office. I picked the lock and made the copy while he was away last night.''

"Nice work. You'd be hot shit in high school, getting copies of tests, changing everybody's grades in the computer. You could make a bundle, chief.''

"I wish life were still that simple. Where the hell *was* Akins last night, anyway?''

"New Orleans. Ben said he had quite a time! Almost lost him twice. Ben doesn't think he made him, but he sure as hell was going out of his way to make it hard to follow him. He met two men in a hotel restaurant. Ben got some conversation on tape, but I couldn't do anything with it. Tran is going to enhance the sound; maybe we can pick something up.''

"Who were the two men?''

"Don't know. Ben got a couple of pictures, but we're waiting for Colonel Milford to get us photos of our hit parade, to see whether we come up with a match.''

"I know Tran's got a lot to do, but tell him to hurry. I got a feeling we're running out of time. Akins has gone over the edge since Jimbo got his throat cut. He's finding an spy under every dead leaf in the woods. Traitors and Communists, Zionists and provocateurs everywhere, he says. Sometimes I'm not sure he's coherent.''

"I almost don't blame him. I mean, pretend for a minute that he's just an ordinary guy trying to put something together. You have something like that happen right under your nose, you'd spook, wouldn't you? Now, you do the same thing to a paranoid crypto-Fascist, and you just set the clock on a walking time bomb. Us black folks can relate to that sort of thing, you dig?''

"Tell me about it.''

"Do yourself a favor, though, would you, Luke?''

"What's that, Cal?''

"Don't tell him you have a piggy bank. He thinks you're an international capitalist, you're dead meat."

"I wish that were more absurd than it sounds."

"You mean it isn't?"

"Uh-uh. Look, we may not see each other for a while. It looks like I'm going to be tied up for a few days. If Akins's big move is in the works, he may not come back here at all. Tell Ben to stay with him, and try to keep Tran posted. With Akins gone, it will be easier to call him."

"You be careful, Luke. I don't like the feel of this whole thing. And these fucking Army intelligence types are driving me up the wall. I wouldn't be surprised to find a couple of them in this stew somehow."

"Don't worry about me and Jake. Just take care of yourself."

Steeples slipped back into the woods without a sound. A moment later Luke found himself wondering whether he'd been there at all. The nightmare of Akins's camp was coloring everything he thought, and everything he did.

Luke headed back to the barracks like a man walking in his sleep.

Back in the lab, Tran felt like a man given a reprieve from the governor. Never at ease in the concrete jungle of a large city, he preferred the solitude of the desert and the company of blinking diodes. Steeples had given him enough raw material to keep him busy through the night.

Not knowing where to start, he crammed a couple of betel nuts in his mouth and nudged the heavy brass cuspidor closer to his desk. His first job was going to be tedious, but it had to be done. He'd already sent the film upstairs to the lab for development. While he waited for it he decided to test a new interface program he'd been tinkering with.

Spreading the photocopy of the computer list on his desk, he checked the pages quickly. Some of the images were a little blurry, and he cursed the poor quality, knowing this wouldn't be the best test but hoping it would be good enough.

The idea was simple. With a small video camera he was going to scan each page in succession. The video signal would be run through a filtering program, converted to a stream of digital data, and automatically dumped to the computer. It seemed simple enough, but he'd never tried it before.

Tran sighed, picked up the printout, and attached it to a tractor feed. He checked the camera settings, refined the prism calibrations to limit the video input to a single line of printout, pushed the "start" button, and prayed.

The clicking tractor feed was the only sound in the lab. As it hauled the paper through, the camera, synchronized to the rate of paper flow, imaged each line. If it worked, he'd be spared the enormous job of inputting the huge volume of material by hand.

Once he was satisfied that the mechanical aspects were functioning, he walked to the computer console. He could open the file while it was still in the process of creation. He called it up and watched the screen. It flickered, then snapped into a tight image. He held his breath and waited. Chewing nervously, he looked for the cuspidor, aimed a tight stream of reddish-black juice, and smiled as it sailed home, right on the money. It was a good sign.

The screen began to flicker again. The signal was breaking up. He checked the cable feeds, snugging the monitor jack home, and turned again to the amber face. This time he saw what he had hoped to see. Line by line, text had begun to appear on the screen. As the camera continued to image additional lines on the photocopy, the file grew, scanning down until the screen was full.

Almost hypnotized, Tran watched each line vanish off the top of the screen to be replaced by a new one at the bottom. He stepped back to the camera and adjusted settings to increase the rate of the tractor feed. Back at the screen, he confirmed that everything was still in sync. That left him free to tend to other business.

In one corner of the lab, a soundboard, as good as anything in a modern recording studio, lay silent behind thick glass. Tran grabbed the cassette Ben had given him and walked through the glass door and into the soundproof room. He pressed the button for the lights and waited while the fluorescents kicked in.

Tran slipped the cassette into a dubbing deck and made

three high-speed copies. He took the original and locked it in a small safe over the console. Sitting at the board, he fitted a pair of earphones to his head, dropped one of the copies into the main board, and turned it on. He couldn't process the tape until he knew the condition of the original.

He played it back twice, straining to hear scraps of the conversation. The ambient noise from the restaurant where it had been recorded was deafening, compared to the sound of real value. The first task would be to remove as much of the noise as he could, then he could turn his attention to the enhancement process.

Working with a sophisticated equalizer, Tran isolated the narrow-frequency range of the conversation. Working in increments, he wiped range after range on either side of the conversation.

By playing the altered tape back and boosting the volume, he was able to pick out scraps of intelligible conversation, but there was still a considerable amount of work to do. The main obstacle to be overcome was the presence of other conversation in the same band width. This couldn't be eliminated as easily as the other noise. And doing it wasn't going to be the quickest thing he'd ever done.

The next step was enhancing the remaining content of the tape. This was done by converting it to digital form and selectively boosting the signal. Tran played the revised tape back, listening carefully. Before he was finished, he felt a hand on his shoulder. He turned without removing the earphones. Dave Parker, from the photo lab, was grinning at him. Tran stopped the tape and yanked the phones off.

"New Van Halen?" Parker asked. His innocent smile was more infuriating than the interruption.

Tran spat at the smaller studio cuspidor and missed by several inches.

"You need practice, Tran. You're losing your edge."

"You better have something for me." Tran warned. "If you came down here just to hassle me, I'll show you a kind of edge you've never seen."

Parker smiled. "I know better than that. Yeah, I've got something for you. The microfilm and those candid shots Ben took. It looks like a crummy restaurant. Tacky decor. And the light is lousy."

"Are they usable?"

"With yours truly on the developer? Absolutely. They're not even dry yet, but I thought you'd want to know. I kept buzzing on the intercom, but when you didn't pick up, I thought I'd come down and catch you sleeping on the sofa."

"Sorry to disappoint you."

"I'm glad, actually. It anchors my faith in human potential to know there is at least one man who can go through an entire lifetime without ever closing his eyes."

"I'm not that bad."

"Almost, Tran. Almost. You've already cost me three assistants, damn good ones."

"I'm sorry. But I can't be responsible for your poor choice of assistants. Anyway, shall I come up for the photos?"

"Your call. I'll bring them down as soon as they're dry if you have something to do here. If you want a quick look now, come on up."

"Thanks, Dave."

"No problem," Parker said. He reached into his hip pocket and withdrew a handkerchief. With a delicate, almost parental gesture, he leaned forward to wipe some wayward juice from Tran's chin.

"Christ, you geniuses are all the same," he said with a laugh. "You'd starve to death if somebody didn't bring you a sandwich once in a while."

CHAPTER 22

Luke sat on the edge of his bunk. His nerves had been frazzled for two days. The sun was just beginning to break through a thin overcast. He looked at his watch, noting the time almost absently. It was the fourth time in less than an hour that he'd done so. Sitting and waiting was not his style, but he had no option. The ball was in Marshall Akins's court. That he would serve was certain. What it would be was anyone's guess.

Luke lit a cigarette and tossed the pack onto his pillow. He walked to the front door, debating whether to stay inside. The angry rasp of insects was normally a deterrent, but in his present state, slapping at mosquitoes at least had the virtue of being something to do. It wasn't exactly taking the bull by the horns, but he was going stir-crazy.

He pushed open the screen and moved to one end of the porch, dropping into a hammock suspended from the porch supports. Watching the command hut, he noticed a light on in Akins's office. For a moment he thought about walking over to see what was going on, but he felt too drained to make the effort. If the next move was up to Akins, and it was, the best thing he could do was sit on his hands and be patient.

Before he could make up his mind, Luke noticed a figure

in the doorway of the command hut. The light was still too dim to see who it was. Luke took the last drag of the Marlboro and tossed the cigarette in a glittering arc. The butt landed with a hiss in a shallow puddle. The screen door of the command hut banged open, and the figure stepped out onto the porch.

Moving to the edge of the porch, the figure suddenly took on character, and its features faded in, like a sinister shadow in a movie fog materializing out of nothing. Marshall Akins was on the porch.

Luke watched Akins, who lit a cigarette, took a quick drag, then flipped the butt out and away. Luke climbed out of the hammock and Akins waved. He stepped onto the damp earth, his feet squishing and slapping in the mud and puddles of the clearing.

When he reached the center of the clearing, Akins waved again. "That you, Simmons?" His hoarse whisper seemed to hiss and crackle in the morning stillness. Rather than answer, Luke stepped off the porch and crossed the clearing.

"You're up early, Simmons."

"Couldn't sleep."

"A lot on your mind, eh?"

"Not enough on my mind, actually. It's pretty boring around here."

"Tell it to Jimbo."

"I don't think he'd hear me."

"Well, hold your water. Things are going to liven up pretty soon."

"I've been hearing that all my life. I'm getting too old to pay attention anymore."

"You want something to do, don't worry. I've got the perfect solution."

"What's that?"

"I'm leaving in an hour. Somebody has to run this place for a few days."

"Me?"

"Who else?"

"What about Randall? He's been around a lot longer than I have. He knows everybody. The men seem to like him."

"No argument. But I don't want a popularity contest. And I don't think Randall has the brains of a newt. But you're different. I saw that right away. And I liked the way you disposed of our recent, rather bloody, problem. You seem to understand power, know how to use it."

"Power never interested me very much. I'm not very ambitious."

"That's why you're perfect for the job. You can handle things while I'm away, and you'll be happy to give it back as soon as I return."

"I'm not sure the men will like it."

"I don't care what they like or don't like. This operation is perilously close to coming apart at the seams. If you can hold it together for two or three days, everything will change. I'm putting the finishing touches on something that will turn this country on its ear."

"Oh? What might that be?"

"You'll see when the time comes. I can't afford the risk of telling you now. I don't trust anyone; I'm sure you've noticed that. And I have a strong suspicion that someone in this camp is leaking information to the feds. I can't afford that, either. But until I know who it is, I'm going to have to play a little poker."

"You've been doing pretty well so far."

"Pretty well is small potatoes. I want the whole ball of wax. There are dozens of groups like this one around the country. Everybody thinks he can be the boss. Everybody has the solution to all our problems. I think so too. That would make me just like all the others, except for one thing—I'm right. And all I have to do is prove it. I do that, I'm cock of the walk."

"If you say so."

"Don't worry about Randall. I'll tell him you're in charge. He might grumble a little, but he won't give you any trouble."

"And if he does?"

"Kill him."

"Just like that?"

"Just like that."

"The last man who bought that line got his throat cut."

"But you're not like the others, Simmons. I know it. I can feel it. There's something about you that I can't explain, but I know it's there. I don't think you even recognize it. I admit, I didn't trust you at first. Like I said, trust is not something I can afford too much of. But I'm willing to go with my gut feeling on this one."

"And if you're wrong?"

"I've been wrong before. I'm still here."

"We're all survivors, Akins, or none of us would be here."

"You just do what I say and you won't regret it."

"What about you?"

"What about me?"

"Will you regret it?"

"We'll see, won't we? Besides, your friend, Mr. O'Bannion, will be going with me. You wouldn't want to do anything to jeopardize him, now would you?"

CHAPTER 23

Ben dropped back about a quarter of a mile behind the small convoy for a while. The first reaction from the range finder had taken him by surprise. Things had been quiet for so long, he didn't believe Akins was ever going to leave the camp. Now, rolling through the northern Louisiana country-side, watching the farms slip by on either side, Ben wondered why he had been so anxious to leave the stakeout.

A convoy of air-conditioning trucks seemed anything but earth-shattering. Still, there was more of interest to the con-voy than the crummy art on the side of the trucks. Maybe he was right to want to check it out.

Boredom hadn't been the problem. It couldn't be, not for a man who spent days at a time watching the sun rise and set. Being an Indian policeman was not the world's most glamor-ous occupation. Nor, most times, was it the most dangerous. It left him plenty of time to contemplate his navel, the state of the world, the origin of the universe, or the Padres' chances in the current pennant race. For Ben, who had the Native American's tolerance for things as they are, the latter was often the most perplexing question. About baseball he could get passionate. Maybe he could find something just as inter-esting in the innocuous-looking caravan.

Regaining his resolve and his passion to explore the unknown, Ben cruised up past the remaining trucks, then dropped in behind Akins's blue Lincoln. He was eating gasoline at a pretty good clip. Ben's Camaro had a large tank, probably eighteen gallons, but the modified engine was hungry. The needle was hovering just above half, and it had been full when they started out.

Content to sit in the Lincoln's shadow, Ben considered his options. At the first opportunity he was going to check in with Tran to see if any progress had been made on the maps Luke had copied. He wondered whether any of the men, including Luke or Jake, was in the rear of the trucks. If so, this might be the big move Luke had been waiting for.

His choices weren't particularly striking, but reacting was always a game for those with patience, and Ben had an abundance. He could stay with the trucks, which at the moment seemed like the only sensible course, or he could try to figure out where they were headed and try to beat them there, which seemed unacceptably risky. If he lost them, he might never find them again.

An hour later his gas tank nudging the *E,* he caught a break. The Lincoln pulled into a rest area, stopping at the gas pumps, and the driver got out to talk with the attendant. Ben pulled up to the self-service island and cranked the pump. His engine had been running hot, and he popped the hood to check the oil. It was down a half, but he let it ride. The coolant spillover was full, so the radiator was all right.

The driver got back into the Lincoln while Ben was still topping off his tank. The car spurted out of the service area, and Ben was about to finish when he noticed the blue car nose into a parking space in front of the Howard Johnson's restaurant.

Watching from the corner of his eye, he saw the driver and Marshall Akins both leave the car and head for the door. A moment later a third man left the Lincoln. He wore shades against the bright sun, but there was no mistaking the man's bulk and the way he carried himself. Jake O'Bannion was along for the ride. Something about his demeanor suggested he was less than thrilled about it.

When Jake, too, vanished inside the rest stop, Ben screwed the gas cap back on, paid the attendant, and got in. A space two cars down from the Lincoln was vacant, and Ben jumped out of the car. Akins and the driver were just leaving the men's room as Ben walked into the building. Jake was nowhere in sight. He watched them enter the restaurant, then ran to a phone booth against the far wall. He closed the door with one hand, dropping a quarter with the other. Tran had better be available.

Keeping an eye peeled for O'Bannion, Ben dropped the quarter. So intent was he on his surveillance, he was startled by the harsh clang of the quarter bell.

"I think Akins fucked up, that's what I think." Randall was leaning so close to Luke, the stubble on his chin resolved into individual whiskers.

Luke pushed back his chair and stood up. "I didn't ask you what you thought, Randall."

"Well, I'm telling you, anyway."

"Look, I didn't ask for this. I was as surprised as you are."

"It doesn't make sense. He doesn't trust you. I know that for a fact."

"Look, you want to run things, do it. But you tell Akins when he comes back."

"When's that?"

"I don't know. He didn't say."

Randall threw up his hands in exasperation, turning to the ceiling as if in supplication. "I don't know. He didn't say," he mimicked. Luke thought for a minute that Randall might stamp his foot like a spoiled four-year-old. Finally realizing he was getting nowhere with Luke, he stormed out. "We'll see what the other men have to say about this."

Luke walked to the door and watched Randall stalk across the clearing to Barracks-One. He banged the screen door behind him, as if he knew Luke were watching.

Slipping a dangling hook into its eye, Luke locked the screen door and walked back to the desk. He sat down heavily, sighing in unison with the cushion of the leather chair. He stared at the top of the desk, pointedly ignoring the telephone at one corner. His instinct was to contact Tran, but too many things argued against it. The line was probably bugged, and even if it wasn't, Akins would surely spot the strange number on the phone bill when it came. That presupposed another bill would arrive before this was over. There was just no safe way to do it. At the moment he couldn't afford to leave the camp and would almost certainly be followed if he did.

While he was mulling over his nonexistent range of options, he heard a rap on the screen door. He looked up, but the man in the doorway was all shadow, outlined against the glaring sun behind him.

"Come in."

"I can't. It's locked."

Luke stood and stepped around the desk. As he got closer to the door he recognized Junior Riley. He flipped the hook out of the way and stepped back.

Junior yanked open the door. "Got a minute?" he asked, stepping inside.

"Hell, I got nothing *but* time." Luke was unable to disguise the frustration in his voice. He walked back to the desk and sat on its front edge.

"What can I do for you, Junior?"

"I don't know. Nothing, really. I mean, I just thought maybe you might need some help."

"What kind of help?"

"I don't know. I mean, Andy is over in the barracks stirring up a hornet's nest. He's really pissed off that Akins left you in charge."

"I know." Luke watched the younger man closely.

"He's gonna make a mess of trouble for you."

"Let him. He'll have to answer to Akins. I don't give a rat's ass."

Riley shrugged. He walked aimlessly around the room before speaking again. "How come you're here, Lou?"

"What do you mean? I'm here because I believe in what Heartlanders is doing, same as you."

Riley looked unconvinced. "I don't believe that. Hell, half

the guys here—me, included—are in it for the paycheck. I
guess some of them really believe all that garbage about the
federal government and black people and Jews and . . .''

"What's your point?"

"I dunno. I guess what I'm saying is, I don't believe all
that shit, and I can't believe you do, either.''

"That all?"

"That's about it."

"Well, Junior, don't worry about it. We all have reasons
for what we do. What they are is nobody's business. Maybe I
don't like all the neo-Nazi crap lying around in the barracks.
Maybe I don't like the white supremacy angle, either. But
whether I do or not, it's my business. If you don't like it, that's
your business.''

Riley shrugged again. "Whatever you say, Lou. I just
thought, you know, maybe . . . You know anything about
Tyler Hamilton?"

"Who?"

"Tyler Hamilton. Know who he is?"

"No, can't say I do. Never even heard the name before.
Why, who is he?"

"Oh, hell, I don't know. Just somebody comes around
once in a while. Never here, to the camp. But he shows up
someplace, usually over near Lake Salvador, and Akins runs
like his Daddy's calling. He don't usually stay too long, but
he sure don't look too happy when he gets back. I can tell
you that much. He usually busts our hump for a couple of
days, like Hamilton was giving him Patton lessons or
something.

"You ever see Hamilton?"

"Just once, for a couple of seconds. He was in a car, and I
seen him when the door opened. The glass was dark, you
know, like on them expensive cars, so I didn't get a real good
look.''

"Would you recognize him again?"

"Hell, I don't know. What the hell difference does it
make? The less he comes around, the easier things are around
here. I hope to Christ I never see him again, nor Akins,
neither. Fact is, I was thinking—''

"Junior, don't think. That's the worst thing you can do around here. But you ever see this Hamilton again, you let me know, okay?"

"I don't know, Lou. You try to buck that bastard, he'll cut your gizzard out and eat it. I didn't see much of him my own self, but I heard plenty about him—more than my share, if you want to know the truth. And I seen them eyes of his, like holes in his face. There ain't nothing even there."

"Maybe we can straighten him out a little, next time he shows up."

"Forget about it, Lou. Not me, and not anybody else around here, neither. You need any help with Randall, you can count on me, all right? But you start messing with Hamilton, I'm gone, man. I'll be in Oregon before you hit the fucking floor. I mean it."

"All right, understood. Thanks."

Junior turned and walked toward the door. Luke called after him, and he stopped without turning. "Junior, as far as I'm concerned, this conversation never happened."

Junior nodded wordlessly before pushing open the screen door and letting it bang closed behind him. Then he stuck his head back through the door.

"I knew that," he said, "or I wouldn't never have said nothing."

CHAPTER 24

Jake was uncomfortable sitting in the jouncing truck. It was empty, except for the two men in the cab, and its tight springs, designed for a much heavier load, were bouncing him around. He'd been using the passenger-side mirror to keep track of Ben but tried not to be too obvious about it.

The Arkansas state line was four miles away, and it was certain they were going to head north, up Interstate 65. Pumping Dave Carhart, normally more talkative than a drunken magpie, had proved useless. He either didn't know where they were heading or wasn't prepared to say.

As they skirted Pine Bluff, Jake began to wonder whether there was something more insidious about Ferris being connected to the Heartlanders than he had previously suspected. But the small town was still a hundred and fifty miles away, and the taciturn driver was next to useless as a source of information.

The small caravan highballed it straight into Little Rock and threaded its way through some streets arguably too narrow for such bulky vehicles. In a near deserted industrial area they stopped in front of a huge cotton warehouse. The building appeared to be deserted, but Akins hopped out of his

Lincoln and walked to the left of a rusted corrugated-metal rolling door.

A moment later the door grated and began to rise with the grinding sound of seldom used metal rollers. Akins waved to the lead driver, and the truck lurched in, just clearing the still rising door. The other trucks and the Lincoln followed, and Akins stood talking to a fat man in dirty coveralls. Akins pushed the button to close the door, and they were virtually wrapped in gloom. A small scattering of overhead fluorescents, most with only two of their four bulbs lit, did little more than accentuate the darkness.

Akins and the fat man talked animatedly, but they were too far away for Jake to hear what was being said. It seemed less an argument than an urgent conversation. Jake started to walk toward them, but Carhart grabbed his arm.

"Wait a minute. Marshall don't like nobody listenin'. He wants us to know something, he'll come tell us."

"I was just curious, that's all. We've been on the road a long time. I wanted to know where the hell we were going."

"When we get there, you'll know, won't you, Jake?"

"I don't know if I can wait that long."

"Seems to me you're curious about a lot of things."

"Like what?"

"You been sneaking around the base, you and that friend of yours, since the day you got there. I seen you by the motor-pool shed a couple of nights ago. What were you doin' there, checking the mileage?"

"Why don't you mind your own business," Jake snapped. His nerves were already frayed to the breaking point. He didn't need some backwoods bully pushing him too hard.

"Well, now, see, here's where you're lucky. Anybody else would prob'ly just go tell Marshall you been nosin' around places you shouldn't oughta be. Me, I like to handle things my own self. So, I'll tell what I'm gonna do." He turned to face Jake squarely, his lips drawn and curved into a parody of a smile.

"What might that be, sport?"

"You one ugly son of a bitch. I think I'll give you the benefit of some expert plastic surgery. No charge."

The driver stepped forward, leaning into a roundhouse right with his full weight. Jake sidestepped the punch easily. It was apparent the bigger man had relied on his superior size in most of his fights and was no match for Jake's more graceful approach.

As Carhart careened on by, this momentum given a boost by Jake's well-aimed chop to the back of his neck, he slammed heavily into the side of the truck. A dull echo reverberated through the empty warehouse. The driver turned, shaking his head groggily and cursing under his breath.

Ever the gracious opponent, Jake waited for the man's head to clear, then stepped in, driving a quick combination into the driver's midsection. The stomach, not as flabby as it appeared, thumped as each blow landed, and Jake tossed a quick left jab, catching Carhart below the left eye. The driver's head snapped back, slamming into the truck door handle, and he slid down like a side of beef.

Jake, breathing deeply, stood over the fallen man, waiting for him to rise, when he felt a hand on his shoulder. He turned to stare into the puzzled face of Marshall Akins.

"What the hell is going on here?" Akins was livid.

Jake laughed. "Nothing much. Old Davey, here, was trying to explain something about plastic surgery, I think. You'll have to ask him when he wakes up."

"Jake, I don't need this kind of shit right now. If you can't get along with the other men, I'll have to do something about it right here and now."

"Look, this tub of guts started it. I know I'm the new kid in town, and I don't mind taking orders. But I'll be damned if I have to take a bunch of crap from everybody who knows you longer than a month. You don't want me along, say so. But if I'm part of the team, then I get the same respect as everybody else."

"Of course, of course. You'll have to forgive David. He gets a little rowdy now and then."

"I don't have to forgive anybody anything. Just keep this fat fuck out of my face and we got no problem. He tries anything like this again, I'll take his goddamn head off. You can tell him that when he wakes up."

Jake walked away without looking back. A grimy glass door stood to the right of the large freight door, and Jake headed straight for it. He was stepping through when he heard Akins call him. Jake ignored him.

He stepped out into the bright sun, blinking against the harsh sunlight. An old Coke machine stood alongside a wood-slatted bench that hadn't seen paint at least since Lincoln had made his last trip to the theater.

Jake planted himself in front of the machine, noticed a can of Coke was a dime, and couldn't believe it. He fished in his pocket for some change and hauled out a palmful of small coins. Selecting a tarnished dime, he dropped it into the coin slot and pressed the red button next to the Coke sign. The machine's innards groaned, something heavy rattled around and landed with a thunk. Jake reached into the receptacle, yanked out a can of Patio orange soda, and popped the lid. It wasn't what he'd ordered, but it was cold and it was wet, so he didn't give a damn.

Downing half the can in one gulp, he heard the glass door rattle behind him but didn't bother to turn around. He sipped again, more slowly this time, and moved to the bench, where he sat down, careful to avoid the few obvious splinters jutting up from the naked wood.

Marshall Akins took a seat next to him. Jake said nothing, content to wait Akins out, let him sweat a bit. Finally Akins laughed. "You sure put old Davey to sleep, Jake."

"A good nap never hurt anybody."

"What's eating you, Jake? You seem like you got a seat full of fire ants."

"I guess I just don't see what this is all about. I'm half cooked in that damn truck, bouncing across the country to God knows where, some asshole at the wheel with a thirty-five-word vocabulary. It's tiresome, is all."

"Carhart's all right. He doesn't talk much because he doesn't have anything to say. He means well. And he believes in what we're doing."

"What *are* we doing? I thought this was all about helping the underdog, saving farms, saving jobs."

"Jake, you got to understand things are different out here.

You're used to New York. The pace is faster, there's more people, and more kinds of people. If you catch my drift.''

"I'm not sure I do.''

"People out here like to be with their own kind. They believe, as I do, that God meant each to be with his own. You take a man, a white man, he's worked a farm all his life. Maybe it's been in the family five, six generations. Now he can't make a go of it so well. He knows there's something wrong, but not what it is. He doesn't see how the federal government is taking money out of his pocket and food off his table. And why? So some lazy good-for-nothing can share it with him, bleeding him dry on welfare, all without doing a lick of work to earn it. It ain't his, but Uncle Sam is giving it to him, anyhow.''

Jakes continued to stare straight ahead.

"Now, if you look at things closely, see clearly, you got to figure there's only one reason for it. Jews and Communists have taken over. They want to pollute the American people, mix the races, and all so they can get rich and take over the whole country.''

"The way you lay it out, they already have. What chance does a bunch of pitchfork soldiers in dirty overalls have to beat a combination like that?''

"They're American soldiers, Jake, with American pitchforks. We plan it right, we can take back what's ours. And, by God, that's exactly what we're going to do.''

"Sounds like a tall order.''

"I didn't say it wasn't. But we have resources, and we have help. More help than you might think. There are people in the government, in a position to help, who are doing just that. All we need is a little cash. We get our hands on some money, we can buy whatever we still need. If we have to wage a guerrilla war, so be it. I've been there before. I was in Special Forces in 'Nam. Trained the Montagnards. Those people knew how to fight for what belonged to them. I don't see any reason we can't teach the white man in this country to do the same thing. Hell, the slopes weren't any smarter. They just knew what they wanted. Soon as somebody showed them how to get it, they were right there, raring to go.''

"I don't see any tractor convoy lining up behind you."

"Not yet, but you will, Jake. You will. You can count on it." Akins laughed self-consciously. "I was going to say you can take that to the bank, but that won't be the safest place for anything you want to hang on to. Not for a while, at least."

"Tell me something, Akins."

"Sure. Long as we're chatting friendly like, why not?"

"What happened to Pete Marcelli?"

Akins stared off at the sun for a long moment. He reached for Jake's orange soda and drained the can before answering. "Jake, I'm trying to do something important, call it's God's work if you will, or trying to restore the American dream, rekindling the spirit of patriotism, reclaiming the country for those people for whom it was originally intended . . . whatever you want. I guess, in a way, I'm doing all of those things. Not alone, of course, there are others who think like I do, who see how badly things have gone, but somebody has to stand up and do something about it. I don't know if that makes me special, but I sure as hell know I'm doing special work."

"What's that got to do with Marcelli?"

"When you have a delicate mission, one that requires precise attention to detail, obedience, discipline, you can't afford to tolerate any disruptive influence. Marcelli was out for himself. He didn't give a good goddamn if blacks and whites married. Hell, he even had a nigger mistress for a couple of years. And he wouldn't follow orders, wouldn't listen to reason."

"So you killed him . . ."

"Not me, no. But I didn't disapprove of what happened to him. Jimbo did it, and he paid the price for it, too, but I'd be willing to bet he'd do it again, if he had to do it all over. See, Jimbo was everything Marcelli wasn't. Jimbo had a mission. He knew what was wrong and what had to be done about it."

"And what exactly does have to be done?"

Akins stood up and walked to the soda machine. He dug a dime out of his neatly pressed jeans pocket and dropped it into the slot. When the soda clattered out into the receptacle, he grabbed the can and rubbed it across his forehead. Rather than return to the bench, he leaned back against the machine.

"See, this is what America used to be like, Jake. Soda for a dime. Two thousand dollars for a car. A young husband could buy a twelve-thousand-dollar house for five percent down. But no more. Marcelli didn't give a damn about that. As long as he made a few bucks, money to spend on his whores, he didn't care what happened to the rest of us, to the real Americans. That bothered me, and it bothered Jimbo. I don't know how many times I warned him, but he kept on pushing. Well, it was time to push back . . . and I pushed."

Jake kept shooting glances up the block. The nose of Ben's gray Camaro was just visible at the next corner. He hoped to Christ the sound equipment was in place and functioning. He knew Ben had one of the latest laser mikes, but it was no good out-of-doors. A directional shotgun would be a hell of a lot better, but it wasn't easy to use without being conspicuous. That was the one thing neither of them could afford.

Every time he thought about the possibility of discovery, he saw the clotted, gaping throat of the zealous patriot who managed to get his throat cut for his troubles. Jake was determined not to end up like Jimbo Robinson.

"Jake, I know you don't understand everything I'm trying to tell you. Or maybe you do, and you disagree. All I ask is that you stick with the program. Watch us, meet a few of the others . . . then make up your mind. The Klan, see, they're old hat. Time has passed them by. All those sheets and grand dragons and that kind of horseshit. It's a joke. But the Heartlanders, now, we're different. We're for real, Jake. We got a job to do and we're going to get it done. No matter what it takes."

"Shit like you're talking about doesn't come cheap, Marshall."

"In two days it won't matter. You wanted to know where we're going. Well, I make it a rule never to tell anybody more than one step ahead. All I'm going to say is that we have a secure location, just under the Missouri border, near a town called Ferris."

"That was Marcelli's Waterloo, wasn't it? The bank robbery."

"You might say that. See, we have some friends there, in the sheriff's department. Men who think like we do. They can give us a hand now and then. And they make sure nobody gets too close."

"You mean to tell me you have the sheriff on your team?"

"Not that sheriff, no. Son of a bitch got himself elected passing for white. But there's deputies on our team. And we have a lot of law officers around this part of the country. They might not be on the team, but they're comfortable on the fence, at least. There are one or two pains in the ass. That mulatto, Hodges, is one. But I can handle him. There's another guy, a couple of counties over, don't like us too much, either. But we got some help in the state police up there in Missouri. And by the time we get finished with our next move, we won't have a thing to worry about. I guarantee it. Like the commercial used to say, Jake, 'Try it, you'll like it.' "

"I guess we're heading to Ferris, then."

"Pretty close. Be there by nightfall. I think you'll be more than a little surprised. So will Simmons, when he finds out what the next move is."

"And . . ."

"All in due time, Jake. All in due time. Let me worry about things. That's why I've been chosen. And as you know, there's a lot more called than are equal to the task. But if there's one thing Marshall Akins isn't, it's a shirker. I know what has to be done. And, by God, it's gonna get done right. You just watch."

CHAPTER 25

The three trucks appeared out of nowhere. Luke heard the noise, looked out the window, and slammed through the screen door onto the porch. Andy Randall was already talking to the driver of the lead truck.

"What's going on?" Luke demanded.

"You tell me, big shot. You're in charge, ain't you?"

Luke had opened his mouth to respond when a crackle of heavy static interrupted him. The lead driver reached down under the dash and handed something to Randall. It looked like a modular phone, but it resembled nothing sold over the counter. Randall sneered, then handed the receiver to Luke.

"It's probably for you."

Luke snatched the receiver and put it to his ear. He heard a swirling sound, as if a ghetto blaster were being played in a washing machine. The puzzled look on his face broke Randall up. "All right, Bobby, kick in the descrambler. It's too important to jerk around with this asshole anymore."

Randall moved in next to Luke while the driver bent down a second time, reached under the dash, and flipped a small toggle switch. Suddenly, as if the man were standing right next to him, Luke heard the voice of Marshall Akins.

"Simmons, you listening to me?"

"Yeah, I'm here. What was all that noise?"

"That was high technology at its most utilitarian. A mobile scrambler. Don't ask where I got it, because I won't tell you."

"Surprise, surprise."

"The trucks ready to roll?"

"Hell, they just got here. Roll where?"

"Get the men—and I mean all of them—in those trucks and haul ass. We're going to make our move."

"That's just great. Do you mind telling me where our asses are to be hauled?"

"Bobby already knows. You ride with him. Tell Andy to stay in the rear truck. I want everybody in uniform. Anybody stops you, anybody wants to know what's going on, you're just a bunch of survival enthusiasts playing war. Make sure there are no weapons in the truck. You should be here in eight hours, give or take a half."

Luke sighed heavily. "Anything else?"

"Andy giving you a rough time?"

"Did Cassius Clay have fun with Sonny Liston?"

"Good. It'll toughen you up a little. Simmons, you want to be a leader of men, you got to be able to whip the toughest of them. You only have to do it once. Everybody else gets the message. Saves a lot of wear and tear, know what I mean?"

"I'm starting to get the general idea."

"Good, I'll see you in eight hours. Make sure you're on time, understand?"

"Just one problem."

"What's that?"

"Suppose Bobby dies, has a heart attack, or I rip his lungs out, you know, enforcing discipline and all. How will I know where to go?"

"Simmons, you got a real wiseass streak in you, anybody ever tell you that? Anyway, Andy knows where you're going too. At least he knows where it is. You have any problems, just tell him the Farm. He'll know."

"Got it."

Luke handed the receiver back to the driver. He turned to

Randall, who was standing to one side, smirking. "Any message for me?" he asked.

"Just one," Luke said. He stepped back a few paces, then motioned Randall over.

"What's the message?"

Luke swung from the heels. The roundhouse left caught Randall on the point of the chin, and Randall fell like a cement Cabbage Patch Kid. He lay on the ground for several seconds, not moving.

Bobby jumped down out of the truck and ran to the motionless figure. "Christ, I think you broke his neck. . . ."

"He'll be all right. When he wakes up." Luke smiled. "Bobby, get the men from Barracks-One, I'll get the others. Tell them to wear their uniforms, but no—and I mean *no*—weapons are to be brought along. I want them in rank and file alongside the trucks in five minutes.

Bobby looked up at Luke, his face confused.

"You heard me, man. Now move it!"

When Bobby sprinted for the barracks, Luke knelt alongside the prostrate Randall. Slapping his cheeks, he shook the man roughly by the shoulders. "Come on, Randall, wake up."

Randall groaned. He propped himself up on stiff arms, shaking his head to clear it.

"Can you hear me, Randall?" Luke asked.

"Yeah, I hear you fine." He groaned again and got to one knee.

"Now listen and listen good. I don't want any more shit from you. I'm in charge of this unit until we rendezvous. You understand?"

Randall said nothing. Luke slapped him sharply on the forehead with the butt of his palm. "I asked you a question."

"I fucking understand, you bastard. That good enough for you?"

"Just fine. You're riding in the cab of the third truck. Maybe you better go sit there until you wake up."

"Don't patronize me, motherfucker. You might be in charge now, but when we see Akins again, buddy, your ass is gonna be mine."

"I'm warning you, Randall. You give me one more problem, I don't give a shit how small, and you won't live to see
Akins again. You got that, *buddy*?"

Randall climbed unsteadily to his feet and staggered along
the row of trucks. Climbing into the cab of the third and last,
he slipped off the running board, banging his knee on the
steel ridge. He cursed loudly, but like a catcher nicked by a
foul tip, he refused to rub it. Finally hauling himself in only
by force of will, he slumped back in the seat. Luke smiled,
then sprinted over to the other barracks.

Tran listened carefully to the revised tape. It wasn't perfect, but he felt he had done everything possible, within the
limits of available technology, to squeeze its secrets out. This
was his fourth pass, and bit by bit it was falling together.
Fragments were still unintelligible, but he had been able to
reconstruct some of the missing elements by contextual refer-
ence. The process was not nearly as easy as he would have
wished, since the three men were guarded, speaking ellipti-
cally, and verging on unintelligibility by employing short-
hand references only the remaining two men at the table
would understand.

None of them referred to either of the others by name. A
voiceprint of one of the men, however, despite its fuzziness,
matched favorably with that of Marshall Akins, taken from a
recording of one of his speeches.

Tran couldn't identify either of the others. This time, though,
he scratched busily, jotting down names and other key words.
None of the names was personal except for one: Lou Simmons. Tran knew Akins was referring to Luke and was
relieved that neither of the others reacted in any unusual way
at the mention.

It was clear that a plan, one they knew intimately and
apparently had been responsible for constructing, was being
modified as a consequence of events they had not foreseen.
Recriminations were exchanged rather acidly for several minutes until one of the two unknown men took charge. Tran was
amazed at how easily he bent the others. He didn't raise his
voice, and he didn't threaten. Like a trick done with mirrors,

it was all modulation. The man, obviously used to being in command, accomplished with tone what volume could never hope to achieve.

Having gleaned as much as he could from the tape, Tran turned to the Cray. Punching in the key names and phrases, he ran a quick sort to see whether any of the names matched any of those on the lists Luke had managed to copy. None did, and Tran stood up, disgusted.

He paced around the laboratory, this time playing the tape back almost as white noise, letting its monotonous drone and hiss fill the air while he walked off his frustration. He had only one possibility left.

Running a file directory, he found the file he was looking for and punched it up. Street names, seven of them, had appeared in both the conversation and in the detailed maps Luke had found in Akins's office. Whatever else they were talking about, they were certainly concerned with something requiring an intimate knowledge of a major metropolitan area. But why should they spend so much time talking around a set of streets in a city they didn't mention and which Tran had not yet been able to identify?

Whatever the reason might be, it was all the more crucial that he determine what city had been the focus of the maps. The hand-drawn maps were useless in that respect. The detailed, printed maps were something else again. They looked like United States Geological Service maps, but the typical USGS coding was absent. Without it, it wouldn't matter whether it was of USGS origin or not. He couldn't very well call Washington and read the map to some witless telephone functionary and hope to get an answer.

His own atlas, prepared at Luke's request, was extensive but far from complete. A match was possible, but it would take some doing—and more than luck. Imaging the grid on Luke's surreptitious copy, Tran ran it through the Cray and dumped it to a monitor, where it glittered in soft green against a dark blue background. Now come the audacious part.

Cracking his knuckles like a party pianist about to launch into his first number, he leaned back and stared at the screen for a moment. Postponement wasn't possible, even if he were inclined to try it. He typed quickly, asking the Cray to match the image on the screen with any set of lines with a plus or minus five percent degree of variance permitted.

The twittering of the computer sounded almost petulant, but Tran recognized that interpretation as a product of his own guilty conscience. He turned in his swivel chair and watched the banks of LEDs wink on and off. He closed his eyes almost all the way, and the garish display transformed itself into a glittering mosaic, like a brilliant night sky in a galaxy on the other side of the cosmos.

After what seemed like an eternity, the second monitor winked once, then asked whether Tran wanted a list of possibles or a printout of each possible grid. Tran groaned, then settled for the list. So instructing the computer, he listened to the printer snarl line after line, holding his breath until it stopped. Now he would see whether the hours had been worth it.

CHAPTER 26

The farm was idyllic, or would have been, if Jake knew why he was there. The place had come as a complete surprise. The three trucks, disguised as air-conditioning delivery vans, had stopped in a small box canyon at one end of the farm.

Sitting in the cab of the lead truck, Jake was convinced they had made a wrong turn. When the taciturn driver leaned on the horn once, and then again, Jake was certain Carhart was suffering from a Joshua complex. But the canyon was no Jericho. The walls didn't tumble; they moved with a startling massiveness more appropriate to *1,001 Arabian Nights* than to the Bible.

When a huge section of the seemingly solid wall began to rise, Jake's jaw dropped. When the truck, followed by the two others, pulled inside a cavern yawning off into an inky infinity, despite the elaborate lighting overhead, he felt compelled to push it closed again with his hands.

The trucks rumbled ahead, their big diesel engines rattling the solid walls and sending showers of stone chips clattering onto their roofs. A quarter of a mile into the cavern, the driver pulled into a tight turn, leaving the van parked against a solid wall. He jumped down, leaving the engine running, and Jake was right behind him.

Close examination of the wall showed the unmistakable marks of rock drills and pickaxes. Small chips of granite lay at the base of the wall.

Jake tilted his head back, and the high ceiling took his breath away. Nearly sixty feet above them, it was nothing but a looming shadow lurking behind the banks of six-foot fluorescents suspended on chains. The only thing like it Jake had ever seen was a SAC hangar in North Dakota, a building large enough to handle B-52s while a stilt walker painted the big bombers' tails.

He had been impressed with Akins's approach to things, not for its philosophy but for its thoroughness. There was no arguing with the man, or with his commitment. His resources, though, were another matter. Even Goldfinger didn't have the financial wherewithal to carve this hideaway out of solid rock. That left the crucial question unanswered. And like the old days, on *College Bowl*, it was a two-parter—where the hell did he get the kind of money this took, and who had been giving him the kind of assistance that even money couldn't buy, at least not on the open market?

"This is some setup," Jake said, marveling.

"Hell, you see it as many times as I have, it don't even faze you. I been here a dozen times, at least. And you ain't seen the half of it. Akins is one smart son of a bitch. You look at this place from above ground, you got no idea it's here. Hell, you'd need a geologist with a seismograph even to detect this chamber. As you might expect, we ain't had one get too close in a long time now."

"One did, I gather?"

"Uh-huh. One did. He's in a box downstairs."

"You mean there's a prison here too?"

"I said a box, man, not a cage. He done disappeared, man. It was in all the papers. I think the University of Missouri even named a scholarship for him. You know, lost his life in the pursuit of scientific knowledge. Some bullshit like that."

"What do we do now?"

Jake noticed that the other drivers and their passengers had disappeared, almost as soon as they'd left their trucks. He was beginning to feel uneasy.

"I don't give a damn what you do. Akins'll be here soon. You can do what you want till then, as far as I'm concerned. You want to freshen up, I'll show you where to go."

"Yeah, I think I would."

"Let's go, then, before those bastards use all the hot water." Without looking back, the driver made for a steel door set in the wall. Jake hadn't even noticed it until the driver reached for the handle to yank it open. It moved easily on well-oiled hinges, its motion broken by a large pneumatic hinge bolted to the top. The door was already starting to swing shut again when Jake followed the driver through.

What he saw beyond the door was, if possible, still more amazing. If he didn't know better, he'd have sworn he was in the bowels of a large corporate headquarters. Neat corridors stretched to the left and the right and dead ahead. Every wall was broken by an occasional door, but there wasn't a sign in sight. Jake hadn't a clue what lay behind any of the doors.

"You better stick close, O'Bannion. You get lost down here, it might take a few hours to find you. I don't think Marshall's in any mood to send a search party out after some half-assed recruit."

"I'm not exactly a recruit anymore, you know."

"Right, and my father was Thomas Jefferson. Do us both a favor and don't argue. Just do like I say until I get you set. After that you can do anything from read a book to cut your own throat, for all I care."

"You mean, like Jimbo? Was that his problem, boredom?"

"That bastard. Hell, if ever a man deserved killing, he'd have been the main contender, if he didn't already have the title."

"You sound like you're glad he's dead."

"Oh, I am, I'm glad as all get out. I never liked him, and I didn't trust him, either. Not as far as I could throw the state of Missouri, which, by the way, is about fifty feet in that direction."

Carhart pointed down a dark hallway with a quick gesture.

"Far as that goes," he continued, "I don't trust you, either."

"Why not?"

"There's too much about you . . . and your buddy Simmons . . . that I don't know. And what I do know doesn't add up all that well. Not that I'm a whiz at math. But you check my ass, you'll notice there ain't a mark on it. I keep it covered."

"I'll remember that," Jake said, trying to disarm the undertone of hostility in the man's attitude with a smile.

"You do that, O'Bannion. You just do that. You get the kind of scars I'm talking about, you might not sit down again. Ever."

"Maybe you better just point out the showers and turn me loose."

Jake felt better after freshening up. He wasn't crazy about wearing fatigues again, but at least they were clean and smelled like something that hadn't spent several days on a barnyard fence. Prowling around the deserted corridors of the underground facility, he peeked into several offices. Most were just that—small rooms with filing cabinets, desks, and a couple of chairs. A third of the way down the corridor, just visible in the left-hand wall, a heavy steel door jutted out from the soft green walls.

Cocking an ear to see if anyone was nearby, Jake ran down the hall on his toes, trying to make as little noise as possible. The door itself was a single sheet of metal painted dark gray, rimmed with thick rivets every four inches around the outside edge. Presumably a second sheet of steel lay behind the surface of the door. A single handle jutted out slightly, and Jake gave it a tug. To his surprise the door swung open easily, on well-oiled hinges. It opened all the way and lay flat again the wall. The room was dark, but Jake noticed a small array of dull green LEDs glowing in one corner.

Groping along the wall with one hand, he found a light switch, flipped it, and flooded the room with a pale luminescence. Stepping cautiously inside, he reached back to pull the door closed behind him. He gave the perimeter of the room, where the walls and ceiling met, a quick scan, but as far as he could tell, there was no television surveillance equipment installed. In a facility so obviously secret, this puzzled him until he realized that security for the entire installation was so tight, Akins must have felt confident that no one without authorization would ever get this far.

Crossing the concrete floor on tiptoe, he approached the bank of small green lamps. A sophisticated computer array was up and running, although inactive at the moment. For one of the few times since he'd met the diminutive Vietnamese, Jake wished Tran were with him. Computers were as alien as Martian bicycles to the former New York cop. Reluctantly he seated himself on one of three swivel chairs arranged in a straight line before the electronic marvel.

His fingers twitched nervously. Jake was dying to poke at the keyboard, but he knew only enough to know he would almost certainly make a mistake and have security all over his ass before he even realized what he'd done wrong. Standing again, he walked to a printer at one end of the computer station. It was on but not printing. A thick sheaf of fanfold paper lay in the printout receiving tray, and Jake flipped through it casually, taking care not to disrupt an arrangement in some way that might give away his little visit.

He was about to put the paper back into its tray when something caught his eye. Several diagrams, some in three-dimensional sections, had been printed out. One page in particular caught his eye. It looked familiar, but he couldn't place it for a few seconds. Then it hit him—it was the same grid depicted on the map Luke had copied in Akins's Louisiana base office. He had no idea what it represented, but he knew it was significant beyond question. You don't find such a detailed arrangement in two locations unless it mattered to the man who controlled both those locations.

The three-dimensional cross sections were more baffling. They seemed, in a way he couldn't put his finger on, to relate to the grid. But until he knew what the grid showed, there was no point in racking his brain for the connection. He tugged a small camera from the rear pocket of his fatigue pants and made a series of photos, quickly sifting through the documents to find anything that looked significant, concentrating on the three-dimensional renderings and the grid.

He froze for an instant, certain he'd heard someone in the

hall. He stepped quickly back to the doorway and flipped off the light. Holding his breath, he stood by the door. There was no doubt about it. Footsteps were drawing closer.

Flattening himself against the wall, just beyond the light switch, he froze. A sudden rectangle exploded in the wall, and a shadowy figure stepped through. Whoever it was had no interest in the light switch and started to cross the floor toward the computer.

When the man was halfway there, Jake slipped out and tiptoed down the hall. He reached the end of the corridor without incident, turned left, and soon found himself confronted by a short wall with two elevators. Shrugging, he pressed the call button on the nearer elevator, and the door hissed open. Jake stepped inside and pressed "up."

With the familiar pneumatic rush, he found himself zipping toward the surface. The car jolted to a standstill, and the door opened without assistance from him. It was dark outside, and Jake stepped through the doorway gingerly. Holding the door open with his foot, he groped along the door frame, looking for the control buttons. There were two, and they seemed not to have locks on them.

The elevators were set in the wall of a small cave, and Jake felt the damp stone with his hand until he came to the mouth of the cave. Once out in the open, he noticed a small stand of trees in the moonlight. Beyond it, he could see the glimmer of reflected light from the surface of Bull Shoals Lake. Its tangled bank and convoluted contours were an enigma masquerading as a wilderness.

Stepping toward the trees, he heard voices. They were chatting in soft tones, and Jake moved closer to listen. As he got within twenty yards of a clump of chinaberry trees, he recognized Marshall Akins. He could even see the man's silhouette among the sparse trees. The other man was too well shadowed to be recognized. Jake crept closer.

What he saw didn't make him happy. There were two additional men, both arguing quietly with Akins. One, his voice a little too cultured and his vocabulary too expansive for Jake, was a complete stranger. The other man was the problem.

It was Red Dawkins. The last time Jake had seen him, he was sitting behind a desk in Sheriff Leroy Hodges's office. Wearing a deputy's badge.

CHAPTER 27

Jake was fearful of being seen. As it was, he'd already taken too many risks. Backing away carefully through the sparse foliage, he made his way back to the small cavern that concealed the elevator door. As he stepped inside, he groped for the switch to open it. His reaching hand encountered something soft, like cloth, which he didn't remember being there when he'd left.

Fingers, like steel bands, locked around his wrist, and he was twisted sharply to the left and backed against the wall. The bulk pinning him to the rough stone was considerable. Jake struggled to break free, but the hands holding him were too powerful and too expert. The element of surprise had settled the struggle before it had begun.

The grip loosened somewhat, and a weight pressed heavily against him. His captor was obviously using his considerable bulk to pin him while he freed one hand, letting go of one wrist. He heard a brittle rasp that sounded familiar, once and then again. He couldn't quite place it until a small flame erupted just to the left of his face, close enough for its heat to sear his cheek slightly.

"Jake? Is that you? What the hell are you doing out here? How did you find the elevator?" Junior Riley rattled off his

183

questions in a single breath, his bafflement making his hurried interrogation nearly unintelligible.

"Junior? What the hell are you doing? Let me go, for chrissake."

"Sorry. I didn't know it was you. I didn't want anybody to know I was here." His arm moved, almost surreptitiously, and Jake barely caught the glint of an exposed blade in Junior's hand. Next to the lighter, it was what had given him the difficulty in striking the flame. Something flashed through Jake's mind for a brief instant, but it was too bizarre even to consider. Then the blade was gone and the lighter vanished into a shirt pocket.

"How come you're out here?" Junior repeated.

"Just takin' the evening air, lad. I get claustrophobic sometimes. It feels like a prison down there."

"Why don't I believe you?"

"I could ask you what you're doing here too," Jake snapped. "Couldn't I?"

"Sure you could."

"And you'd lie to me, wouldn't you?"

Junior didn't answer immediately, as if it were a philosophical question deserving deep concentration rather than an obvious jibe at Junior's self-serving interrogation. He sighed once, then said, "Yeah, I guess I would."

"Well, there you have it, Junior. We're both here, both of us know it, and neither one of us is willing to tell the other why. How about we call it a stalemate and let it go at that?"

Before Junior could answer it, a pair of headlights stabbed through the trees. Neither man spoke as they watched a large American sedan jounce across a rutted track and turn into a tree-tangled side road. A moment later it was little more than a pair of rapidly dwindling taillights.

"You know who that was?" Junior asked.

"Partly," Jake answered.

When he didn't volunteer who, Junior let the subject drop.

"I guess we better head back inside before somebody wonders where we are, huh?"

"You'd know the answer to that better than I would, Junior."

Jake had reached again for the elevator switch when another pair of headlights slashed through the trees, this time approaching. It was higher on the road, and Jake assumed it was a truck, but the darkness of the tree-shrouded road, even with the moon overhead, was too murky for him to be sure. Almost immediately another pair of lights appeared, some fifty yards behind the first, followed by a third.

"Looks like we're getting company, Junior."

"Yeah. I was wondering when they were going to get here."

"Who?"

"Simmons, Randall, and them."

"All of them?"

"Hell, yes. All of them. I come up by jeep a little while before they left. The whole fucking camp full. Everybody's invited."

"What for?"

"I guess we'll find out in the morning." The elevator arrived and the door hissed open. Junior stepped inside, holding the door open with one beefy hand. "You coming?"

"Not yet. I'm too restless to sleep, and too curious to ignore the new arrivals. I'll be down later. Just do me a favor and make sure nobody locks the elevator down there, would you?"

"I'll try, but I don't have a key."

"Just do what you can."

"All right. Don't be too long, and whatever you do, look out for the sensors."

Jake jerked his head around. "What sensors?"

"You know, them little things that can see you move. Like MacNamara dropped all over Vietnam. They're supposed to alert the guards below."

"I remember them. Hell, even a squirrel going by would set them off. Shit, I think I killed more small game in 'Nam than I did Charlie."

"Well, be careful. Once the trucks are in, the system will be turned back on. A deer goes by, or a rabbit, the guards'll be up here in a flash. They'll blow you away before they bother to ask who the fuck you are."

"Thanks for the tip."

Junior took his hand away, and the elevator door whooshed softly closed. When he was gone, Jake stepped cautiously out of the small cavern again, watching the trucks slowly approaching. The first one stopped in front of the hidden garage door and tooted twice. The door opened, and all three trucks roared in. Unlike the others, these three were painted in standard-issue olive drab. They looked like nothing so much as troop carriers.

Jake thought he recognized Luke sitting in the cab of the first truck, but the light was uncertain, and the truck stationary for too little time. As the big door swung down, Jake knew the time had come to make some kind of a move. Standing in the darkness, he saw the dim figure of a man, intermittently lit by swatches of moonlight as it passed in and out of the trees. Intrigued, Jake held his position and watched the figure's progress. The movement was familiar, but the moonlit silhouette was too amorphous for him to draw any conclusions.

Too impatient to wait any longer, Jake left the security of his hole in the rock and started to creep forward, keeping low and choosing a path that would intersect that of the stealthy shadow.

Finding some cover in a clump of bushes, the big Irishman waited. His nerves were on fire, and his heart beat palpably in his chest. The figure was twenty yards away now, and moving almost straight toward him. Jake cursed his failure to ask Junior where the sensors were planted. If he was inside the perimeter, he could move with some safety; if not, both he and the shadow could be in big trouble. At five feet, as stealthy as an Indian, the man stopped and listened. Jake wasn't sure whether it was innate caution or if he had inadvertently made some sound picked up by the stalker.

Apparently satisfied, the figure began to move forward again when Jake pounced. His rush was headlong, a sumo wrestler's bulk with none of its grace. He barreled into the shadowy figure and knocked him to the ground, immediately falling on top of him and pinning him.

The man struggled for an instant, then muttered, "If that's

you, O'Bannion, I'm going to make you regret it for a least a year."

"Ben?"

"Who the hell do you think?"

"What are you doing here?"

Jake rolled to one side, and the embarrassed Apache sat up. "As usual, I am the bearer of bad tidings for the white eyes. If you and Luke thought Custer had problems, you ain't seen nothing yet."

"What do you mean? What the hell is going on?"

"Tran has figured out what's going down."

"And what might that be?"

"You know that map Luke copied? It's downtown St. Louis."

"Missouri?"

"You know another one worth mentioning?"

Jake bit his tongue.

"And the names he picked off that tape I made in the restaurant? They weren't people. And they weren't places, either."

"So?"

"They were streets, man, St. Louis streets. And they just happen to bracket a rather interesting building."

"Come on dammit, speak plainly for once in your life."

"I trust you've heard of the Federal Reserve Bank? Well, the map is a detailed grid of the area around the bank. The other drawings and charts just happen to show the system of underground tunnels, storm drains, cable channels, wiring conduits, and such. And like a spiderweb, they radiate out from the bank. Tran thinks they're going to try to blow the bank wall from underground, and the paperwork sure looks like he's right."

"Christ. How the hell can the three of us stop an operation like that?"

"It's four, because Calvin is here. And it's more than that, because I had a very interesting meeting with a friend of yours earlier this evening."

"Oh?"

"Jo Mason is one fine-looking woman. It didn't hurt that

she's friendly with one Leroy Hodges, Sheriff of Marion County. It seems the sheriff has been interested in this little farm for quite a while. He also knows no farm worth its salt doesn't bother not to raise a crop, so he's had a deputy watching the place.''

"Maybe so, but that won't help too much."

"Why the hell not?"

"Because one of his deputies was just in the woods not three hundred yards from here, talking to none other than Marshall Akins.''

"You mean, the sheriff is in on it?"

"No. He's too decent a guy. But he already told me he doesn't trust his deputies. They sympathize with Akins and some of the groups like his. Hodges tries to interfere, I'll give you five-to-one odds he has his hands full with his own men. He won't have much left to help us with.''

"He's going to try."

"We can't wait. There must be fifty men downstairs, and everything ripped off from the Ozark Armory too. Everything not used in the Ferris bank robbery, anyway. And God only knows how much firepower they already had stored here. It's like a goddamn armory all its own down there. And if you know an easy way in, I'll eat my shoes.''

"How are you going to get back inside, you overweight leprechaun?"

"Elevator. In a small cave in the rock back here." Jake pointed and Ben looked, even though the area Jake indicated was pitch-black.

"Let's say I believe you, just for the sake of argument. Why can't I go down with you?"

"Because somebody has to stay up here and go for help. And even if you did, it would still be three against sixty or so.''

"Calvin can handle going for help. And I always did like long odds. Let's go. We have to tell Luke as soon as we can, then figure out what the fuck we're going to do about it, although I think I already know what he'll say."

"And what might that be?"

"Simple, actually. When you want to kill a snake, you cut

off its head, right? All we have to do is take Akins out of circulation and we're halfway home."

"I'd almost buy it, if I knew who the other man with Akins and the deputy was."

"You didn't say anything about a third man."

"Yeah, he was there, and I don't have a clue who he was."

"It's got to be the inside man, the contact man of whoever is helping Akins from the federal side."

"Talking about it here won't change anything. We're wasting valuable time," Jake said. "Come on, let's get down before they miss me."

"I can't imagine even your mother missing you." Ben laughed.

Jake led him to the cave and reached for the button. This time the door opened without surprise, and they stepped in. Keeping Ben out of sight was not going to be easy, but like Thelonious Monk once said, "Worry later."

CHAPTER 28

Jake stepped out of the elevator. The corridor, now more dimly lit than it had been, was deserted. In the dull light it seemed even longer than it was. He whispered to Ben, "You wait here. I have to find someplace we can hide you until I find Luke."

"We don't have much time," Ben whispered.

"Why not?"

"I told Calvin that if I wasn't back in two hours, he should come looking for me."

"Christ Almighty. With those sensors up there, the guards will spot him for sure. They'll cut him to pieces before he gets within two hundred yards of the main exit. You got a radio on you?"

"Yeah, but there's no way it'll make it through three hundred feet of solid granite. Not with all the steel reinforcements in this place."

Jake nodded. He waved Ben deeper into the recesses of the elevator. Walking quietly on the balls of his feet, he reached a right-angled intersection. Both branches were deserted, but the left was more dimly lit. It seemed like the best bet. He walked down the hall trying the first two doors he came to, but they were locked. The third knob turned easily, and Jake pushed the door open.

It was pitch-black, but he couldn't risk a light until the door closed behind him. When it hissed shut on pneumatic hinges, he reached for the door frame, traced it quickly with his fingers, and found a bank of switches. Holding his breath, he clicked the first and nothing happened. Doing the same with the second, he was rewarded with a burst of light.

What he saw staggered him. Jake looked up to the thirty-foot ceiling, and the topmost crate of row upon row of stacks barely cleared the pre-stressed concrete ceiling. He knew what was in the boxes. He didn't need to check the serial numbers to know where they'd come from.

It was the Ozark Armory cache. He'd known all along it was here somewhere, but it was a lot more than that. Crates of ammunition and weapons of every variety were stacked in veritable mountains.

But the more important problem at the moment was to get Ben securely hidden. He clicked off the light and worked his way back to the elevator, keeping close to the corridor walls. Two surveillance cameras were mounted at the intersection, but they didn't seem to be working, so he ignored them. A moment later he hauled Ben bodily out of the elevator and hustled him down the corridor.

Pushing him into the magazine, he closed the door and flipped on the light. A quick scan of the room turned up a desk in one corner, a small gooseneck lamp bent almost to the desk surface, its red metal shade too garish by half in the drab surroundings. Jake turned on the lamp and signaled Ben to shut off the overhead fluorescents.

"You wait here. I know how you hate hanging around, but I have to get Luke before we do anything. We're in this together. We get separated, they can use us against each other. I'll be back as soon as I can."

Without waiting for Ben's answer, almost certain to be an argument, Jake slipped back into the hallway and moved quickly toward the sleeping quarters. If Luke was anywhere in the underground complex, it would be there. With any luck he'd be alone.

In the sterile, dormitory-style living quarters, a few men lounged on Spartan bunks. Others were busy checking equipment, cleaning weapons, and generally running through the drill, as if a white-glove inspection were minutes away. Luke lay sprawled on his bunk, staring at the ceiling. Junior Riley lay on the next bunk.

Jake stifled the urge to sprint over to his boss, opting for a stiffly casual strut. It seemed to take him forever until he reached the vacant bunk on Luke's other side and dropped down as if for a chat.

"Long time no see, Lou. Where you been?"

Luke grinned. "Baby-sitting."

"When'd you get in?"

"You know damn well when he got in," Junior whispered. "We was both up there when the trucks pulled up."

Jake glared at the big kid. His blondish hair, cut so short that he looked bald, was smeared to one side, like a streaky paste of yellowish moss. Under his lip a feeble, misbegotten mustache was doing its best to harden the babyish features. It shouldn't have bothered. Junior still looked every bit the high-school senior larking about with a big brother and his friends.

"Ease up, Jake, Junior and I have had a long talk. He's on our side."

"I almost believe it," Jake said, sneering. "You must be losing it, Luke."

"Jake, Pete Marcelli wasn't the greatest man in the world. Hell, he was downright mean sometimes. But at least he treated me decent most of the time. He made fun of me, but he liked me. I know he did. What they done to him wasn't right."

"Why don't we talk about it later, Junior, all right? I got something to discuss with Lou is private."

Junior grumbled but left his bunk, drifting down the aisle toward a noisy poker game. He looked back over his shoulder at Jake once, just before reaching the circle of kibitzers, but his face was impassive. Jake couldn't read a thing in it.

"Ben's here," Jake whispered.

"Of course he is. He's been following us all the way from Louisiana."

"No," Jake mumbled impatiently, "I don't mean here, I mean *here*. He's waiting in the magazine. And you'll never guess what else is in there."

"I don't have to. Junior told me all about it."

"He what?"

"I'll tell you later. Let's go talk to Ben. We got a few plans to make."

Keeping Ben between them, Luke and Jake hustled across the busy staging area. The trucks were arrayed in a single rank of six. The three olive-drab vehicles were surrounded by a swarm of men in coveralls. Already the cabs and sides had been sprayed the same dark blue as the three trucks Ben had followed from the camp.

A three-man team had already sketched the outlines of the air-conditioning logo. In a matter of hours all six trucks would look the same. As far as anyone would be able to tell, Kirschbaum Air Conditioning would be having a busy day in downtown St. Louis.

Slipping along the far wall, Luke led the way to Akins's office. The three men from Deadly Force stepped inside. Marshall Akins was at his desk, head bent over a detailed map spread in front of him. He looked up when the three men entered, his gaze lingering a moment on Ben, as if in silent consideration of whether he'd ever seen the Apache before.

"What is it, Lou? I'm pretty busy here. Last-minute details for tomorrow's operation."

"It doesn't matter, Akins. There isn't going to be any operation, tomorrow or any other day. We know what you're up to, and this is the end of the line."

Akins smiled and tilted back in his chair. "So our cards are finally on the table." Lacing his fingers behind his neck, he propped his feet up on the desk, meticulously avoiding the documents occupying most of its surface. "And what, exactly, have I been up to?"

"You want it in chronological order or descending order under the criminal code?" Jake asked.

"Suit yourself."

"Well," Luke said, "we can start with fraud, move on to

theft of government property, murder of two soldiers at the
Ozark Armory, grand theft and bank robbery, the murders of
Thomas Mitchell and William McCallum, the assassination
of David Hammond, the murder of Pete Marcelli . . . Shall I
go on?''

''It sounds quite impressive. You must really think me a
desperado of some magnitude, Mr. Simpson.''

Luke looked startled. Somehow Akins had learned who he
was. No doubt the leak in Army intelligence was responsible
for that, but it was too late for any makeshift plumbing now.

Akins went on, his manner that of a bored professor teaching the same course for the twentieth time. ''But let me set a
few things straight. To begin with, there is no fraud. I have
never taken money under false pretenses and never made any
use of money contributed to me for purposes other than those
for which it had been solicited. The weapons stored at the
Ozark Armory belong to the American people. All of them,
and if the powers-that-be are remiss in looking after the best
interests of their constituents, it is incumbent upon someone
to discharge the responsibilities they have neglected. To that I
plead guilty. The death of the two sentries was unfortunate. I
admit that, but accidents happen. The price of freedom is
vigilance. Sometimes that price is a heavy one. I am sorry
two young men had to pay it, but someone had to. I know
they were only doing their duty, but the fault must then lie
with those who command them.''

''You sound so damn smug, I want to puke,'' Jake said,
snarling.

''Please, Mr. O'Bannion, don't soil my office. If you have
to relieve your nausea, use the lavatory down the hall.''

Jake took a step forward, but Luke reached out to bar his
way.

''Let me continue,'' Akins went on. ''The bank robbery
you refer to, I assume, is the one in Ferris, not so very far
from here. I neither authorized nor participated in that unfortunate event. The man who was responsible has been identified and properly dealt with. So much for the robbery and
grand theft. As to the death of the late Mr. Marcelli, that was
no more than the implementation of the judgment of a jury of

his peers. He transgressed. He compromised an important operation . . . and he was punished. The American system of justice at its most nakedly elemental, don't you agree? And as for Mr. Hammond, I admit he was becoming a major irritant, but I had nothing to do with his rather explosive departure for the next world."

"I suppose you're going to tell me the Grucci family did it," Luke said.

"Very amusing, but no, not at all. And since I don't know who *is* responsible, I am not even an accessory."

"I think we'll let a jury a little more in step with reality make that decision."

"I'm sorry, Mr. Simpson, but I have some important work to do. I can't allow you to interfere."

"Not much you can do about it," Luke said. He stepped toward the desk, reaching for the map at the same time. He grabbed it by one corner and tugged, then began to roll it into a tight cylinder.

"Please be careful of that map, Mr. Simpson. It's the most detailed one I have."

"I already told you, you don't need it because you aren't going to get a chance to use it."

Akins smiled and dropped his feet back to the floor. Their well-polished tips flashed as they passed through the tight arc of light emanating from the small lamp at one corner of the desk. "Andy, would you mind stepping in here a moment? I need a little help explaining the way of the world to Mr. Simpson and his cohorts."

The metallic click behind him told Luke more than he cared to know. He turned to see Andy Randall, followed by four men in fatigues, step through the doorway. Randall's smile was beatific. The mat-black tube in his hand was the sound suppressor of a Uzi submachine gun. His four storm troopers were similarly armed.

Randall stepped briskly to the three new captives and removed the side arm each was wearing. Gesturing with the muzzle of the Uzi, he instructed one of his men to conduct a more thorough search.

"Simpson," Randall said with a smirk, "I told you not to fuck with me, didn't I?"

Luke ignored the question.

"Didn't I?" he repeated, bringing the muzzle up in a vicious arc that caught Luke a glancing blow on the edge of the jaw. He fell to one knee. Jake stepped forward, but a second Uzi, jammed forcibly into his gut, put the brakes on him almost immediately.

Ben Sanchez, still in the middle, said nothing. No one in the room, not even Luke, would have dared to guess what he might be thinking.

CHAPTER 29

The room was a smaller version of the concrete-ceilinged space where the weapons cache was stored. It was naked, save for the four men who stood at its center. Luke faced Akins squarely, and over the man's shoulder he could see Randall in the doorway.

"I'll be back in a few days," Akins was saying, but Luke barely heard him. "If you last that long, I'll deal with you then. If not . . ." Akins shrugged, palms up, to indicate both his inability to prevent it and his indifference to the result. Akins backed away a few feet, turned suddenly on his heel, and was gone.

The heavy steel door banged shut with the finality of a mausoleum receiving its last family member. Jake rushed to the heavy panel, but it had already been fastened. Its seamless mount left little hope to remove it by anything but explosives or sheer force. They had none of the former, and their numbers were too small for the latter.

Without raising his head, Ben said, "We might as well sit down and wait."

"Wait? Wait for what? What the hell good is waiting?"

"I told you, Calvin was waiting two hours, then he was going for help. Two hours is up. That means Calvin will be here. Until he is, we don't have a prayer of getting out of here, anyway. And in case you haven't noticed, a possibility I mention despite its obviousness, there are no air vents in this room. What we have to breathe at the moment is all we're going to get, so why don't you sit down and shut up? We'll all live a few minutes longer.''

"Oh, wonderful, my Native American genius, just wonderful! And how is Calvin going to get in here in the first place? He's not James Bond. Hell, he's not even *Julian* Bond. And if he *does* get in, how the fuck will he find us, lad? Tell me that one.''

"Television, Jake.'' Luke, tired of the bickering, decided to deflect what he couldn't prevent. He pointed to a far corner of the room, up near the ceiling, where a single TV camera was mounted.

"Great,'' Jake said, "only the two I saw in the hall weren't functional. This one probably isn't, either.''

"I'm not so sure, Jake. I've seen a red light go on three or four times, a few seconds each time, since we've been here. I think it must be one of those sequential systems with rotating camera input rather than rotating monitor imaging.''

"It still doesn't get us out, boyo.''

"But Calvin likes to watch TV,'' Ben said. "And he loves *The Flintstones*. No way he'd miss you flipping through channels, Fred.''

Jake laughed in spite of himself. Ben was right. Since there was nothing they could do for the moment, the only thing to do was nothing. Anything else was simply an exercise in futility.

The midnight rumble of the truck fleet was ephemeral. Six stuttering roars drifting off into the darkness, their combined sound was gone off into the night before anyone could get to a window. A half hour later, on Interstate 160, there was no one even to care. The all-night rumble of traffic was a given.

Marshall Akins could hardly contain himself. Sitting in the cab of the lead truck, he was Washington riding into battle against the redcoats. Intent on saving his version of the Republic, nothing else mattered. And when the world learned of his dramatic coup that afternoon, people all over the country would be rallying to the cause. If he did it right, this one battle would win the war.

Every now and then he glanced into the side-view mirror to count the trucks, as if he feared they might be swallowed by some lurking monster stalking and devouring them one by one. Uncharacteristically, Junior Riley drove in total silence, his chattering stilled by something he didn't understand and which Akins failed to notice.

At Poplar Bluff they picked up Interstate 67. St. Louis was due north. The scattered small towns hung like mirages on either side of the road, distant still lifes of clapboard and barn siding.

Unfolding the map and reading it segment by segment on his lap, Akins went over the plan in his head one more time. Like most forcible entries, swiftness was the key. And again, getting out was always the hardest part. For both reasons he had chosen the storm drains and tunnels.

Parking the six trucks at various locations was a bit of ingenuity he couldn't ignore. Who would notice teams of men with toolboxes going underground at the beginning of a work-day? After all, wasn't that what they were for? Weren't they the kind of men who kept things running and who we seldom thought about until things went wrong?

If the rendezvous went off on schedule, they'd enter the subterranean labyrinth leading to the Federal Reserve Bank at two points. Their toolboxes, now no longer camouflaging the M16s, C-4 plastic explosive, grenades, and grenade launch-ers, would lie in the water- and sludge-filled tunnels, rusting away to nothing.

But by then it wouldn't matter. By then the Heartlanders would have struck the one fatal blow needed to bring the whole perverted, banker-dominated federal government to its knees. The Communists in the media would be dumbstruck, the Jews on Wall Street would wring their hands in anguish, and best of all, the niggers would start running for their lives. This was going to be a white man's America again, as God had meant it to be.

And he, Marshall Akins, already had the guns. Soon he

would have the money and the public image. Charisma, they called it, and by God, no one would be more charismatic than he. And wasn't that all you really needed to make things work? Weren't guns and money the poles of power, the battery that made the world go 'round?

Ten miles from St. Louis he started to laugh. As the skyline of the city suddenly erupted on the predawn horizon, he was still chuckling. It was really going to work. He could barely contain himself.

The air was getting thick. Luke shook himself to ward off the effects of diminishing oxygen. For what must have been at least the tenth time, he walked to the door and began to search its edge. The seal was tight. No breeze, no draft, not a breath of air was coming in.

Ben was handling himself, as usual, with a stoic placidity, but Jake was growing more and more agitated. The more he moved, the more oxygen he consumed.

Bending low to check the threshold jointure one more time, he was startled by a thunderous rap on the heavy metal.

"Luke, Jake, you in there?" The words were muffled, as if they had traveled a great distance under water. "You guys okay?"

"Calvin?"

"Yeah. I was getting worried, man."

"The air is getting pretty low in here. Can you get us out?"

"Yeah, but I'm gonna have to blow the fucker off its hinges. I couldn't find a key, and there's nobody here. Stand back as far away from the door as you can. And keep out of a straight line."

The three men huddled in a corner of the room, pressing themselves against the same wall that held the door. Any debris from the blast would be least likely to fly in that direction.

There was a long moment of silence. For the three men it felt like a year. The ear-shattering blast slammed the door, twisted but still intact, into the opposite wall, where it buried itself in the concrete, raining dust and scattering splinters of stone like shrapnel.

The boiling cloud of dust swirled and settled quickly as Calvin stepped through. He was followed by a big man Luke had never seen.

"Leroy, is that you?" Jake shouted.

Hodges smiled. "You city boys ought not mess with country life. It can get a lot more complicated than a shotgun rack in a pickup."

"You knew this place was here?"

"Nope, not for sure. But I was curious. And you can thank your stars Jo Mason has big ears and a sharp mind."

"What are you talking about?"

"She pieced a few things together, first of which was that you weren't what you wanted her to think you were. Then she started hearing things in Ralston's, and she come over to see me. I put that together with what Samantha Tyler told us, and it started to add up. So when this brother shows up in my office, I get the last piece in place. Then me and Calvin put a nice squeeze on Billy Harbaugh, my *former* deputy. Made a kind of pre-Miranda accordion out of the dude. Squeeze a white man hard enough, you be amazed what comes out, ain't that right, Calvin?"

Steeples laughed.

"Now," Hodges continued, "anybody want to sit down and tell me what the fuck is going on here? I got a gut feeling I'm working overtime for a couple of days."

"You got any strings you can pull in St. Louis, Sheriff, you better start yanking," Luke said. "Akins is going after the Federal Reserve Bank. I don't know for sure whether he wants to knock it over or blow it up. But we don't have a hell of a lot of time to do anything about it."

"Sorry, Simpson, you couldn't run a yo-yo on the strings I got to pull. On the other hand, I got some vacation time coming. You take volunteers?"

"Can Walter Payton play football?"

"That's it, then."

"Okay, first thing we got to do," Luke said, "is make sure this place is covered. If we miss Akins and his bunch, or if anybody else knows about it, we've got even bigger problems."

"I already took care of that," Hodges said. "Buddy of mine, Larkin Dennis, is second-in-command of Ozark Armory. He's sending a team over to nail things down here."

"Good work. Now, we have the maps and we know where the bank is, so all we have to do is get there before the fireworks. Any ideas?"

"There's two Cobras in the warehouse," Calvin said. "We can get to St. Louis a lot quicker than them jive-ass trucks. They got a big lead, but I think we can catch them."

"All right, Cal, you and Ben check one of the choppers. Jake, Leroy, and I will scrounge up some weapons. Meet you in the warehouse in twenty minutes."

"Guns ain't gonna be no problem," Jake said. "I know where the Ozark stash is."

"Let's go."

CHAPTER 30

The Cobra was straining. With five heavily armed men aboard
and a full load of fuel, it was pushing toward the outer edge
of its capability. Calvin ignored the formality of a flight plan
and kept the chopper low. Moving flat out, they were doing
one hundred and seventy miles per hour, more than three
times the speed of the fleet of trucks. But the six-hour head
start was going to be hard to make up.

Luke sat with the maps on his lap, trying to devise the most
economical counterattack possible. Close study of the underground channels available, concentrating on those most easily
accessible from the street and offering the fewest obstacles to
successful penetration of the Federal Reserve Bank, narrowed
Luke's choice down to three.

While he studied the charts Calvin patched them through to
the St. Louis police. Colonel Milford was on his way to the
hastily assembled command center, but until he arrived, it
was going to be Deadly Force against a deadly foe. Luke had
no doubt Marshall Akins had drifted over the edge. Failure
was no longer in the man's vocabulary. He had come too far,
done too much, and, most importantly, generated far too
many expectations to back down. Akins would achieve his
goal or die trying. The death of a single lunatic, while

sometimes tragic, is seldom catastrophic. What made this case different was the number of followers Akins had at his command and the nearly incalculable firepower they commanded.

Luke spent several minutes discussing his plan with the SWAT team leader of the St. Louis police contingent. The signal was weak, and Calvin didn't have the ability to patch it through a satellite. The Cobra was the only thing handy, and there had been no time to customize it for their special needs.

The probable points of attack formed a rough triangle. The plan called for heavy police presence kept well out of sight and at all the workable locations, but special emphasis on the three most likely. At the end of the conversation with the SWAT team leader, Milford arrived. He informed Luke that Tran had been able to pinpoint the connections Akins had forged with dissidents in the Army command structure, and the suspects had already been placed under house arrest.

That was both good news and bad. Akins was on his own now, and heavily armed though he was, his resources were finite. That was the good news. The bad news was that as soon as Akins realized the precariousness, obviously terminal, of his situation, whatever vestiges of logic still governed the man's thinking would be gone. It was bunker time for Marshall Akins, and a small war in the very bowels of a major American city was a possibility. Luke was determined to prevent that if at all possible. He didn't want to think about the odds.

As they neared St. Louis, Captain Alexander Neville, the SWAT leader, informed the chopper that all teams were in place. So far none of the air-conditioning trucks had been sighted. Substantial teams of men were well concealed at all locations. The next move belonged to Akins. Waiting was the only sensible course of action.

Neville was under strict orders not to interfere with the Heartlander penetration teams until they had gone underground. While they would still be able, either in desperate vengeance or accidentally, to cripple large parts of St. Louis, Luke wanted at all costs to avoid a major firefight in the downtown area and to contain the damage. The need for secrecy meant pedestrian and vehicular traffic would have to appear normal. It was a risk Luke disliked, but Jake had argued so vigorously for it, there was no other course to be taken.

"How we doing on time, Calvin?" Luke asked the pilot.

Absorbed in his complex responsibilities, Calvin mumbled out of the side of his mouth. "I make it twenty minutes to Smith Park. It's the closest place we can put down without arousing too much attention. And the National Guard Armory is right there, so nobody should notice anything unusual."

"I don't know what Akins's timetable is like, so I guess we'll have to make do with that."

"We pick up a little steam as we burn off the fuel. The ship will get a little lighter but not enough to make a real difference."

"Never mind, Cal, just do the best you can."

"I'll be happy if you get us there in one piece," O'Bannion volunteered.

"Since when you only been one piece, fat man? Word is you buy suits with two pairs of pants and wear one on each leg."

"That's no longer true," Jake said.

"Five minutes, boss," Calvin shouted over the straining engine. Pointing ahead and to the left, he continued, "That's the park. I'm gonna hit the first clearing big enough to put this baby down."

"Do it, Cal."

Marshall Akins grabbed the microphone. Raising the drivers of the other trucks, he barked deployment instructions with a frenetic energy Junior Riley had never heard before. Two trucks were directed to each of the three points of the rough triangle Luke had identified. Receiving a roger from each driver, Akins snapped the mike back into its rack and sighed deeply.

"This is it, Junior. This is the big time. How's it feel?"

"Okay, I guess."

"Come on, where's your esprit de corps, Junior? We are

finally going to pull off the big one. From here on it's all downhill.''

When Junior failed to respond, Akins turned to look out the window in silence. In the side-view mirror he watched two pairs of trucks peel off and begin threading their way to their assigned locations. Traffic on the Chestnut Expressway was heavy but moving steadily. It was a typical late-summer-morning rush hour. Hiding in plain sight, Akins felt like Hannibal crossing the Alps. Surprise, the underdog's best friend, was definitely with him.

The remaining two trucks left the expressway at the City Hall exit. At the designated location a large steel grate covered concrete steps leading down into the labyrinthine tangle of emptiness that underlay every great American city. Akins leaned forward, looking for a parking space. He had deliberately chosen the location not only for the access it afforded but because parking was limited to trucks and delivery vans only. No overzealous traffic cop would have reason to look twice at the van.

They were in luck. Half a block of free curb lay on the right-hand side of the street. The grate was only thirty feet ahead of their front bumper as Junior pulled up behind a stationery-supply van. Killing the engine, he watched the tailing truck pull in right behind him. Eager as a little boy on vacation, Akins jumped to the ground, while Junior sat, hands still on the steering wheel, wondering why he was there at all.

"Come on, Riley, haul your ass out here." Akins sounded every bit the annoyed supervisor.

Junior climbed down slowly, walking on the street side toward the rear of the truck. When he turned the corner, Akins had already opened the rear doors. The five-man team riding in the rear shoved toolboxes and crates toward the tailgate. All were dressed in workmen's coveralls, "Kirschbaum" stitched in dark red against the blue-and-white stripes. The choice of colors escaped Junior, but Akins smiled as he watched the men maneuver.

When everything was stacked on the hydraulic tailgate, Akins threw the handle and watched the heavy weight stutter

to the ground. The follow-up truck was unloading, and Akins
barked a few orders, then strutted to the rear of the second
vehicle. Things were going smoothly. Glancing at his watch,
he realized they even had nineteen minutes to kill. They could
lounge around a bit after getting the equipment on hand trucks
and muscling it over to the steel grate.

Junior grabbed the folding MEN AT WORK sign and lugged it
down to the grate. In his back pocket he carried a large hex
wrench and, after placing the sign, knelt to address himself to
the removal of the bolts holding the grate in place. He
wondered if they were going as well for the other two teams.

As he worked, he kept running over his conversation with
Lou Simmons. The man had said some things that made
sense, more sense then anything Akins had ever said, especially when you stripped away all the rah-rah garbage. Junior
wasn't used to thinking on his own, and he didn't like the
way it made him feel. The helplessness and uncertainty were
unsettling.

Akins climbed back into the truck to check with the two
other teams. Both were in place and had completed unloading. He looked at his watch and counted down the two
minutes remaining. "All right! Go!"

A Cobra gunship passed overhead, and Junior Riley looked
up for an instant, remembering the sound from ten years and
ten thousand miles away. It still gave him chills. He pushed
the memories from his mind and grabbed one end of the
heavy steel grate.

Cal touched down in Smith Park, and three men, bending
low to avoid the rotor blades, rushed toward the chopper.
Luke leapt out as the blades spun to a halt. Colonel Milford
introduced him to Alex Neville, and the three men stepped to
one side of the chopper.

"What have we got so far?" Luke said.

"We've spotted all six trucks. They're all unloaded. There
seems to be seven men with each vehicle. They're working in
teams, opening access to the tunnels, just like you thought.
One team is already underground."

"What about the intercepts?"

"In two cases we were able to get a SWAT team underground and into position between them and the bank. As they go under, we move in aboveground. They're bottled up. The third was no go. We'll have to go in after them."

"And what about Akins, which team is he with?"

"Based on photo surveillance, and the radio traffic, as near as we can figure it, he's with the third team. At least that's where the orders were coming from."

"Then it's got to be Akins's team. Where are they?"

Neville opened a map and knelt down. He scrutinized it for a moment to get his bearings, then pointed with a gloved finger. "Here's where they went under. It's got to be slow going down there. They're lugging a lot of stuff."

"And I bet I know what that stuff is. We better get rolling."

"How many men do you want to take with you?"

"I've already got four of the best, right here. Just get us to the access point, then cover it from aboveground. Put a team in the bank, in case they make it through, and try to cover any side routes they might use for escape."

"That's a pretty tall order, Simpson."

"We don't do it, you might have a mess you don't even want to think about dealing with."

"You got enough firepower?" Milford asked.

"I think so. You get anything from Hamilton that might help us?"

"Hamilton's dead. Cyanide capsule. The guy was a lunatic. He thought life was one big spy novel."

"You know, Milford, the older I get, the more I think he might just be right. There's enough freaks out there to make us all crazy."

Before Milford could answer, the radio on Neville's belt crackled. He opened the mike and held a hurried conversation, more tone than words. Slipping the radio back into its case, he said, "So far, so good. One team surrendered. They were pinched in a blind alley, made a wrong turn somewhere. They had no place to go."

"Akins?" Luke asked.

Neville shook his head. "A second team is exchanging fire

with some of my men. They've got a couple of wounded, but they're dead in the water and they know it. Shouldn't last more than a couple of minutes."

"Looks like Akins's team is all you have to worry about, Simpson."

Luke nodded. "And it won't be easy, I promise you."

"You sure you don't want any help?"

"I'm sure. We'll end up falling all over ourselves down there. Speed is our best bet."

"Good luck."

"Thanks, I have a feeling I'm going to need it."

CHAPTER 31

The hole gaped open, a yawning mouth that Luke knew might swallow them whole. He led the way down the steps, his feet crackling on years of foil gum wrappers, brittle cigarette butts, and the assorted detritus that manages to slip through all the cracks. In a way Marshall Akins was the same kind of garbage. He had slipped through some crack in reality and fallen into another world. But this was no rabbit hole, and Marshall Akins was no Alice. Underground, nothing would be as it seemed, but there was no Red Queen to worry about. If anybody would take Luke's head off, it would be Marshall Akins.

Jake, Calvin, Ben, and Leroy followed him, their boots shuffling through the litter for a few moments until they stepped down into the bottom of the tunnel. Thick water, its greasy surface rainbow sheened in the gleam of their flashlights, burbled under their feet.

Luke took the point and realized their lights made them sitting ducks. He ordered them extinguished and used his own periodically, a few seconds at a time, just to keep track of their progress.

"Look, I think we should spread out a little. The tunnel isn't very broad, so walk two abreast behind me, and at the first sound hit the deck. One burst from a Uzi could take us all down at once.''

Every hundred yards or so, Luke stopped to listen. So far, other than the thickly gurgling water, all they'd heard was the scurry of small animals.

Luke tripped, skinning his shins, and pitched forward into the slimy muck. He cursed and swung around, aiming his light at the obstacle. A red toolbox lay across the tunnel. To one side, the torch picked out a stack of crates, all empty.

''Whatever was in them boxes won't make things any cooler,'' Leroy mumbled.

Luke got to his feet, rubbed his bruised shins for a few seconds, then pushed on. They were nearly halfway in and so far had heard nothing. Luke picked up the pace, Jake puffing along behind him.

Ben slipped up to take a position alongside Luke. ''Maybe you and I should go on ahead. I think we can make better time. The others can follow and cover our asses.''

''I don't know, Ben, there's fourteen men up there, and we have no idea what they're packing.''

''But if they don't know we're behind them, it won't matter. At least we can slow them up until Jake and the others catch up with us. It might buy us some time and save some heavy damage.''

''You're probably right. Tell Jake.''

''I already did. He pissed and moaned about me suggesting he wasn't in shape, but he always does that.''

''Let's go, then.''

Luke picked up the pace. He and Ben started alternating use of their lights to prevent anyone from drawing a bead on a single source. Five minutes later Ben grabbed Luke by the shoulder.

''Listen, I think I heard something up ahead.''

Luke cocked his ears, but his hearing wasn't nearly as sharp as that of the Apache. Whatever Ben had heard could have been anything from a truck passing by overhead to some work in a department-store basement.

''I don't hear anything.''

"Voice, man. Whispering, but angry about something. Let's turn on the afterburners."

Without waiting for a reply, Ben stepped out ahead. Fifty yards later, a light speared out at right angles from the tunnel. Ben stopped in his tracks, listening. That two men were arguing was beyond dispute. About what, and who they might be, was impossible to determine.

Suddenly a blade of light stabbed in their direction. This time the voices were clearly intelligible. "What the fuck are you doing?"

"I think I heard something. Back there." The light played back and forth across the tunnel. At its first appearance, Luke and Ben had dived to the muck beneath them, burrowing down into the slime and sticky water as deeply as they could.

"You're crazy, there's nobody there. Look!" A second light joined the first, spearing back and forth, gleaming on the water oozing from the walls. "Probably a rat, that's all."

"Akins, I'm telling you, the only rat you got to worry about is Simpson."

"Hell, Andy, he's dead by now. There wasn't any way he could breathe for more than a few hours in that room. The Indian and the fat fuck too. Forget about it, all right?"

"Then how come we got jumped? The whole fucking op is blown, and you don't even see it."

"The op isn't blown just because somebody betrayed us. It's a little tougher, I'll grant you, but if we can't pull this off, we might as well pack it in, go on welfare like the leeches we're trying to get rid of in the first place. Besides, this isn't the place to talk about that. We'll hash it out when we get back to the farm."

"You mean *if*, don't you? *If* we get back to the farm? We're down to fifteen men. They got my whole team except me, and all of the other one."

"It doesn't matter. A strong commander has to expect losses. You can't win a war if you're unwilling to accept casualties. Come on, the longer we argue, the worse our chances."

The voice began to fade, and Luke jumped to his feet.

"Let's go, Ben. If we can take him here, we might be able to prevent more bloodshed."

"I'd just as soon blow the fuckers all away."

"Not if we don't have to."

The two men pushed forward, keeping to the sides of the tunnel. They sprinted through the darkness, not bothering with lights. Luke was beginning to feel as if he'd never been aboveground. It wasn't a comfortable sensation.

Their feet slapped the mucky stone, and suddenly the echo bounced off and away to one side. They had passed an intersection.

"Think we should check it out?" Ben asked.

"You go ahead. I'm going to head straight for the bank wall."

Ben felt the opening with his hands and slipped in. It was a smaller tunnel, and he had to bend to keep from rapping his head on projecting stones from the ceiling.

Luke continued on a straight course. A faint glimmer ahead told him he was getting close. Jake and the others would be some distance behind him, but they would follow him, rather than Ben.

The lights grew in intensity, and Luke dropped to the floor of the tunnel. In the accumulated glare he could see a swarm of men, a vision out of Dante, scurrying about. They were handing things to a three-man team bent over at the base of the wall.

Luke crawled forward on his belly, ignoring the slime creeping into his collar and soaking his clothes. He was fifty yards away from the wall, just outside the circle of light generated by the array of flashlights. For a moment he debated calling for their surrender, but he had nothing to back it up if they called his bluff. Fifteen to one were lousy odds. He'd have to wait until the others joined him. He made a quick count and came up with only fourteen. Somebody was missing. He was too far away to see the shadowy faces clearly enough to identify the men. While he waited, he looked for Akins, hoping the man would turn his face into the light.

If there was one single thing Luke was determined to do, it was to cut the heart out of the Heartlanders.

Footsteps behind him caused him to turn. It was too dark to see, but it had to be Jake and the others. The time had come at last. He had turned back to watch the work when he felt a hand on his shoulder. "Get down, Jake. We'll have to pick our spot."

"You got no say in the matter, Simpson." A light stabbed down at him as he turned. He'd already recognized the voice but tried to peer through the glare. The light moved slightly, and the grin of Andy Randall swam into focus. "Get up, motherfucker."

Randall jabbed him in the rib cage with the muzzle of an M16. Luke got to his knees. Slightly off-balance, he couldn't react quickly enough when the butt of the rifle spun toward him, cracking into the side of his head. Stars shot past his eyes for an instant, then he blacked out.

Randall grabbed Luke by the ankles and dragged him toward the circle of light. As he reached the others he let go of Luke's feet. "You were right, Marshall," he said. "It *was* just a rat."

Akins gaped at the unconscious form. "How the hell did he get here?"

"It don't matter. He's rat meat now."

Jake stumbled to a halt, Leroy and Calvin right behind him. Paralyzed, the three men watched the tableau being played out before them. The first move they made, Randall would shoot Luke where he lay. If they did nothing, Randall would probably shoot him, anyway. It was a lose-lose situation.

"What shall I do with him?" Randall asked. His tone suggested he already knew the answer. Randall walked around the prostrate form, savoring the moment and trying to decide the appropriate spot to deliver the coup de grace. Finally he brought the muzzle of the M16 right up against the base of Luke's skull.

"We have to do something," Jake said. "Now! They must have Ben too."

Before anyone could answer, a burst of fire exploded in the

tunnel, its individual shots blurred into one thunderous echo bouncing away down the stony labyrinth.

Andy Randall pitched forward onto his face, his head nearly severed from his body. In the orange light the bloody mess looked like the pulp of a giant pomegranate.

Everyone froze. Marshall Akins was the first to recover. He turned to stare behind him, and Junior Riley had still not lowered his weapon.

"Are you crazy, Junior? What the hell did you do that for?"

Junior didn't say anything. He just stood, as if mute, the weapon motionless in his hands. One of the others stepped toward him, snatched the rifle, and Junior put up no resistance. It was as if the single act of pulling the trigger had drained all life from him too.

Marshall Akins yanked a .45 automatic from his hip and fired twice, point-blank, into Junior Riley's face. The boyish features disappeared in a red blur and he toppled forward, blood streaking the pale smear of blond hair on the portions of his skull still remaining.

"That's it," Jake said. "It's now or never." He jumped to his feet and charged forward, firing his M16 and sweeping the slugs in a tight arc. Right behind him, Leroy Hodges and Calvin Steeples spread out to either side. Jake reached the prostrate form of Luke Simpson and dropped to his knees. A stray slug caught him in the shoulder, but he continued to struggle with Luke's unconscious form.

Stunned at first by the attack, the sporadic return fire of the Heartlanders began to zero in. The roar of automatic weapons, amplified by the confined space, was deafening. The counter-fire was murderous, and Calvin was hopelessly pinned down.

Leroy rushed to Jake's side, grabbed him by the shoulder, then shoved him flat. "You got to stay down, Jake."

A sharp pain slashed through Leroy's thigh, and he fell into the muck. As he lay there, he felt a hand on his weapon. He turned over, ignoring the pain, and saw Luke grinning at him. "This is your idea of a vacation, huh?"

Leroy relinquished his hold on the weapon, and Luke

squirmed toward the wall, dragging Leroy behind him. Marshall Akins, a stark shadow in the orange light, paced back and forth, heedless of the firefight raging around him.

"*Simpson-nn, you bastard-ddd!* Where are you?"

Luke climbed unsteadily to his feet and faced the raging Akins. As if on a directorial cue, the firing ceased.

"Give it up, Akins, it's all over!" Luke said. His voice, flat and toneless, sounded strange to his own ears.

Luke wobbled, and Akins sensed the weakness. He charged forward, the .45 still clenched tightly in his fist. He slipped in the slime and fell forward, crashing into Luke and knocking him down. He stood over Luke, aiming the big Army Colt.

"Drop it, Akins. Believe me, I'd just as soon blow your fucking head off. Don't tempt me."

Marshall Akins looked over his shoulder. Behind him, starkly outlined in the glare, like a figure from hell, Ben Sanchez aimed an M16 at his midsection. Almost as if in a daze, Akins raised the .45. Ben watched him, his finger tensing on his trigger. Akins's gun continued to rise—up to his forehead.

Luke, realizing what was happening, got to his feet. Standing behind Akins, he had taken Ben's clear shot away. He lunged for Akins, but too late. The .45 barked, its sound strangely muffled, and fragments of skull and brain tissue splattered the rocky ceiling above them, the gray matter sticking and now indistinguishable from the slime already on the walls. The bone clattered like small pebbles down into the water.

A large rat, its eyes a dull orange, waited in a recess in the wall.